ARE

an astronaut turned into a machine, and now searching for your stolen humanity . . .

a woman volunteering to be frozen for a hundred thousand years to await the return of your lover . . .

a survivor of a holocaust stumbling over a nightmare landscape toward a dream-like city shimmering in the distance . . .

a new kind of soldier beginning to doubt his mission as an infinitely powerful instrument of destruction . . .

a man hunted by computers through the streets, buildings, and sewers of a vast and murderous metropolis . . .

an explorer returning over time and space to the horror that he still thinks of as home . . .

YOU ARE

an inhabitant,
a slave,
a victim,
an enemy,
a witness of . . .

THE TIME-SWEPT CITY

Also by Thomas F. Monte~~~~ ~~~~leone?

NIGHT THINGS

THE SECRET SEA

THE TIME CONNECTION

The
TIME-SWEPT CITY
by Thomas F. Monteleone

POPULAR LIBRARY • NEW YORK

THE TIME-SWEPT CITY

Published by Popular Library, CBS Educational and Professional Publishing, a division of CBS, Inc.

Portions of this novel appeared previously in the following publications:

"Chicago" FUTURE CITY, Trident Press, 1973, Copyright © 1973 by Thomas F. Monteleone

"Good and Faithful Servant" AMAZING SCIENCE FICTION, March, 1976, Copyright © 1976 by Ultimate Publications

"Breath's a Ware That Will Not Keep" DYSTOPIAN VISIONS, Prentice Hall, 1975, Copyright © 1975 by Thomas F. Monteleone

"Far From Eve and Morning" AMAZING SCIENCE FICTION, October, 1977, Copyright © 1977 by Ultimate Publications

First Popular Library printing: October 1977

13 12 11 10 9 8 7 6 5 4 3

For Natalie . . .
Again and Always

Cities have a life of their own.
Like all living things, they grow
to their own pattern,
not ours.

—Frederik Pohl

ONE

Link had tasted the universe.

He had sifted light-years through his fingers like grains of sand; he had breathed plasma like summer air; he had worn a starbow like a crown upon his head. He had been both starship and man.

Now, only the man remained.

He lay in a hospital bed, in a starkly white room, at the edge of the City which had sent him to the stars and now called him back. He was an amusing puzzle for the machines to ponder as he struggled to recover from a special madness. In the IASA installation, Link lay wrestling with the phantoms of his tormented consciousness. Over and over, his moment of collapse was reenacted.

Link remembered . . .

He slipped into an almost circular orbit. The Earth turned slowly beneath him as he touched its surface with his sensors and auxiliary scanning equipment. Watching and feeling, Link/Ship sensed the small surfaceship climbing toward him, and he absorbed the shortwave communication into his cybernetic receivers: "Commander Link? This is Shuttle

41-C . . . 'Acknowledge please . . . Request permission to begin docking."

The long-feared moment had finally come, and Link/Ship wished that he could ignore it. Instead, he beamed out a short reply: "Affirmative, 41-C . . . I have you on instrument tracking . . . All systems green . . . Proceed to forward docking collar on present course."

As he waited for the small ship's final approach and contact, he felt himself becoming apprehensive, and he fought down a rising swell of panic. He tried to savor the sensations of the cybernetic/biological mix that was himself; whenever he concentrated on the phenomenon, he felt mildly intoxicated. Yet he was still in complete control. With the Ship's electronic sense organs, Link/Ship was a member of a very elite race of beings.

New signals raced into him, jarring him from his private thoughts, which said that the docking collar had been sealed. He opened his airlock and patiently waited for the technicians to scramble into him. Link/Ship heard their footfalls, felt the infrared heat of their bodies, as the men made their cautious way to the bridge. They were coming toward him as he floated weightlessly in the colloidal-suspension tank. He wore a specially designed suit with a small opening at the base of his spine, from which a shining, serpent-like cable led to a terminal on the side of the tank.

Their words invaded his mind: "All ready, Commander Link?"

Turning, shifting around in the suspension, Link/Ship regarded them with his human eyes: they were lean young men, wearing the jumpsuits of the IASA; they were his unwitting torturers. "Yes," he said after a long pause. "I am."

He forced himself to watch as they began the process. One of them inserted supportive waldoes into the tank and cradled his human body firmly. The other one threw some switches on the manual panel and the temperature of the colloid began to change. Slowly it liquified and began to drain from the tank. But at this point, Link/Ship could still feel everything, even the slight electric pulses that controlled the tank's thermostats.

When the tank was empty, one of the technicians climbed in and began manipulating the cable and its coupling at the base of Link/Ship's spine. He felt the gross tampering as the man measured and checked the connection with small tools. Link/Ship watched as the man outside the tank nodded and threw more switches on the manual panel. Instantly, the changes crashed through him. It was slow, inexorable, and painless, but he almost cried out as the cybernetic systems began to shut down. Half of his consciousness was fading, failing . . . dying. Ship-awareness slipped away from him, and he dropped into a vortex of darkness. Link felt as if an invisible scalpel was systematically cutting away the onion-like layers of his self.

Specter-like, the blinking computer displays on the manual panel flickered and died. The last weak pulse of ship sensation touched his mind; and in a moment of imploding darkness, the cybernetic system was down.

Link struggled against the twilight awareness: the small-talk conversation of the technicians, the feel of the close-fitting fabric of
his suit, the thrum of blood passing through
his temples were his only sensations now.

Slowly, he became aware of the mechanical
arms that held his limp body. Then there
were the human hands scampering like crabs
over the fittings of his suit, fumbling with
the catches, opening the seals. They removed
his helmet and the stale air of the bridge assaulted him—he was not prepared for the reality of machine oil and perspiration.

They peeled the rest of the suit from his
pale body and he became conscious of his
lean frame, even though he was weightless.
He felt bitterness and even anger at the rough
way in which they treated him, although he
knew it was necessary to complete the assignment. The technicians, like himself, had no
choice in this matter. Fingers fumbled with
the coupling. Special tools clicked into place
as Link felt them removing the cable. Movement, and the seal of the coupling was violated—the umbilical had been cut—and Link
wrestled with the new psychological pain. He
imagined the cable dropping off, away from
his spine, and instantly shriveling and dying
and falling lifelessly to the bottom of the tank.
Link then saw the man outside the tank reach
into a pouch and produce a round, flat disc.
He handed it to the other technician, who
moved it into position at the base of Link's
spine. Link imagined the coupling there: an
open wound, oozing an invisible life-sub-
stance, a death wound. He felt the disc being

*snapped over the coupling—the bio-connector
—sealing it indefinitely.*

*He knew that his private access to the
voices of time and the stars was irretrievably
gone. Like other men, he was condemned to
flounder in the backwash of his meager human senses. These were his thoughts as the
two technicians carried his limp body away
from the bridge. When they reached the airlock, Link saw the young pilot they had
chosen to replace him: a young, strong-look-
ing man with fire in his eyes. As Link
struggled against the darkness that was raging
in his mind, he tried to speak out to the young
pilot, tried to warn him of what would eventually come.*

*But the moment passed too quickly. They
brought him into the surfaceship and prepared
for the long slide back into the atmosphere.
Link was wrapped in a deceleration web, left
to contend with the fist of madness that
wanted to crush him.*

. . . and tried to forget.

The room, the bed, and the personnel were
now familiar to him. Through the window,
opposite his bed, he was afforded a spectacu-
lar view of the lake and the City of Chicago
beyond it. Watching it, Link knew that he
had come home to an unpredictable future.
He was reminded of how the City's computers had planned everything for him,
prepared for every contingency . . . except
the one that actually took place.

The door opened, and Link watched a
short, somewhat fat, bearded man enter the

room, carrying a medical transcriptor. He wore the uniform of the IASA, but its light green color indicated his physician status. Link studied the man's deliberate gait as he approached the bed. "Good morning," he said, intoning pleasantness with some effort.

"Hello, Herson." Link looked away. He did not want to talk.

"We're not finished with the tests yet," said the doctor. "But from the early data, there doesn't seem to be any physiological damage."

"That's comforting. So I'm just imagining it all . . . is that it?"

Herson ignored the remark. "But we're going to make some more tests—just to be positive."

Link relaxed his body, feeling the tension leave his muscles. He had to admire Herson's patience with him, the doctor's cool professionalism in the face of his madness. "All right, then," Link finally said. "What's wrong with me?"

"We're not sure, of course. But you seem to be suffering from some kind of sensory deprivation." Dr. Herson rubbed his beard absently. "The drugs seem to be controlling it most of the time . . . But we need more time, to be certain. The computers are working on it."

"Yes, I'm okay now," said Link, massaging his temples. "Calm. Rested. But the darkness is still there inside me, just hanging over me. I can still feel it, and it's not going away. It's like half of me just isn't there anymore."

"The chemotherapy should help," said the doctor as he nervously tapped the edge of the transcriptor. "But we've only just started in that area, and I'm afraid that the rest might be up to you."

"Meaning?"

"Meaning that you'll have to cooperate with us. You've got to stop lying here feeling sorry for yourself and decide whether or not you want to live in this comparatively bland world of ours."

Link could only nod in agreement. Herson was as perceptive as he was direct. The doctor had tried being sympathetic, but Link knew that such tactics were useless against death-wish cynicism. Herson's pragmatic approach was far more effective, and even more appealing to Link.

"Remember," Herson was saying, "the choice, in the end, can only be yours."

"Then I really don't have much choice at all, do I?" Link tried to smile, but failed.

Herson did smile, as if in mockery. Standing up, he said, "No, Link, you really don't." The bearded man turned and left the room.

The treatment plan was drawn up, and Link, somewhat to his own surprise, responded as best he could. At Herson's insistence, he did as much exercise and walking as possible. Enzyme injections had prevented his muscles from atrophying while aboard ship, but a rigorous program was still needed to assume complete control again. Gradually he increased his exercises until he was spending several hours each day walking through corridors of the installation. He would pause during these times only to look at the lake from the great cubed building's observation deck. It was so immense—a small sea.

From that height, he could see gentle surf touching the cliffs below. In the evenings, the images of the water were even more captivating; and he longed to be near it, as he had once longed to be near the stars. He felt an affinity to the sea: how it reached, and touched, and finally retreated from the land. It was as if the sea did not wish to come too close to the earth, for fear of being trapped there—as Link was now trapped.

The beach held a special fascination for him. In it, he saw a twilight place—a place where he might stand and contend with the forces that still threatened to overwhelm him. Perhaps the beach was a compromise where solutions could be pieced together. Link's mind, he felt, was standing in a twilight place between sanity and madness, between life and death.

He was thinking more clearly now; Herson's chloropromazines seemed to be working. He no longer feared that the remaining half of his mind would be blotted out like errant ink on a page. The tormented visions had almost ceased entirely.

Almost.

There were still nights when he would wake up screaming into the darkness of his room. The moonlight, flowing through his window, would burn his eyes. The memories of the stars and the wailing light-years would come rushing back, seeking out the cybernetic complex that was no longer there. The hum of the air conditioners became the crackle of ionic storms; the room became the suspension tank and he almost gagged as he fought to keep the colloidal liquid from drowning him. He fought against these attacks—"lapses," Herson had called them—until they eventually faded and disappeared. But he was always left shaking with the knowledge that the specters still lurked within his divided mind.

Days passed into weeks and the lapses grew less frequent. Perhaps the time was growing near when they would cease altogether. Link hoped that this were so, although that fact would only mean new obstacles to overcome. Life still offered him little solace. His talks with Herson seemed to underscore this; and he would still have to choose between a life or a death. It was at this time that he was allowed to walk along the beach. He began looking forward to those times. They gave his life some purpose, and each day he spent more time there, walking more miles, thinking more clearly.

Link noticed an oddity about the place. Perhaps it was the underwater configuration of shoreline, or perhaps it was a particularly strong undercurrent; he was never sure. In the evenings, when the tide went out, he saw that the beach was strewn with the casual debris of life. Along his path, he encountered things which the sea had rejected like unwanted offspring. Usually they were creatures that, once cast out, could not return. Link knew that death patrolled that narrow wet strip of sand. Often, he stood and watched the gulls swoop down ahead of him to feast among the dead and dying creatures of the sea. He heard the screams of the birds, which sounded to him like a final alarm, and perhaps a final solution.

It made him think of the utter unpredictability of the sea and of all living things. Man included. The sea: great wellspring, giver of life, magical. It had spawned life and awareness, and that awareness seemed to be rushing out at him. It came to him from some unremembered primordial center as the galaxies had done, expanding into endless night.

Link felt that he was growing to know some of the sea's many moods and temperaments. (It was actually a great lake, but Link always thought of it as "the sea.") He had seen its storms, which were brief yet fierce affairs. And when they struck, death became an even busier collector along the shoreline. But sometimes, after such a storm, Link had seen other, far stranger types of collectors. They were usually men from the nearby City of Chicago who walked the beaches carrying knapsacks. They looked for the simple treasures of the storm-swept sand: a crustacean husk, a shell, or perhaps a sponge-like thing that once had been alive.

Link had always thought it was a morbid pastime. He envisioned greater beings than ourselves, at some future time, rummaging among the graves of men—looking for a particularly well-turned skull or a curious piece of gristle.

But one evening, having walked farther than usual, Link discovered that he had passed beyond sight of the installation. It was beyond the last point of land and the thought unsettled him a bit, much like the feelings of a small boy who wanders away from his home for the first time. Recognizing this latent fear, he continued walking, since he was determined to regain total control of himself.

Looking off into the distance, Link saw a solitary figure walking along the barren, wind-swept shore. The person's silhouette was framed by the amethyst evening sky, and Link stopped to watch while the wind's fingers combed through his hair and danced upon his face. The person ahead of him seemed to be engaged in some serious and private activity: crouching down in the sand for a few moments, then standing up and tossing something out to sea.

Link began walking again, closing on the figure until he was near enough to see that it was a young woman. The moon was coming up now, and it cast pale yellow veils along the blue isle of night. He could see her clearly in the soft, new light as she moved gracefully across the sand. Link felt something stirring within his mind; a reaction to her aesthetic sensuality. He continued to walk toward her until he was only several meters away.

Turning, she faced him. Her face was a perfect oval, which radiated warmth and serenity. She showed no fear of him and the hint of a smile danced upon her lips.

"It's a beautiful night, isn't it?" she asked.

Link did not reply. He could not. He was so taken with her simple words. Her voice was the soft sound of the sea; it rolled over him and then withdrew, leaving him refreshed.

She turned and began walking again, as if to indicate that Link should follow her. He did this, and they walked for several minutes in what Link felt was an awkward silence.

Suddenly, unexpectedly, she stopped as they approached an object lying on the beach ahead of them. She huddled down to examine it, and Link watched as her fingers lightly touched the quivering body of a cephalopod, washed up helplessly onto the sand. Its slimy skin reflected the moonglow; its solitary eye stared upward at Link. He could almost feel the hopelessness that radiated from that eye.

The girl took the sea-thing into her hands.

Before she stood, Link forced himself to speak. "Do you ... collect them?" His voice was shallow, fraught with tension.

"In a way." She looked up and smiled at him. "But only the living."

Link did not immediately understand the reply. He could only watch as she stood up, holding the limp creature in her right hand. A wave broke on the beach, and she drew back her arm and tossed the large-eyed thing far out into the deep water. It fell and disappeared beyond the breakers.

"Perhaps it will live now ..." she said as she wiped her hands on her faded jeans.

Link looked at her cautiously, not wanting her to know that he was studying her. She was attractive in an odd sort of way. It had something to do with the collection of outstanding characteristics, but Link was not able to articulate it. Her skin was cool ivory; her eyes were large, black pearls, her hair was a raven fall, tangled by the salt spray. He was embarrassed that she should look upon his cracked, star-burned features, that she should tolerate his awkward presence.

"I saw you before," he said finally, aware of the silence but almost sorry that he had disturbed it. "Back there, I mean. When I was coming up the beach."

She nodded and pushed a strand of hair from her cheek.

"Do you walk here very often?" He wished to hear her voice again.

"Oh, yes." She paused and laughed lightly, casting a quick glance out to the sea. "Every night. But not always this beach." She glanced down at the sand. "There are so many beaches along this coast . . . and so many nights."

Link could only nod his head in agreement, although he did not really understand her. He followed her in silence as she began walking again. Entering a small cove, she came upon another beached creature which still glistened with the faint glow of life. Spying it, Link was repulsed by its shape—a blistered, crab-like thing with long, sagging antennae. He stood dumbly as she bent down and picked up the thing in her delicate fingers. Again she threw it back to the dark waters. It made a brief splash of whiteness as it struck the surface, and then it was gone.

Saying nothing this time, she continued to walk, and Link followed. He was struck then as to how futile her mission actually was. No matter how many of them she could save from oblivion each night, he thought, the difference was sure to be slight. She must have known, he thought, that death raced across the beaches of the planet at a pace far greater than hers, collecting more than she ever could.

But he did not tell her this. Instead, he asked, "Do you live close by?"

"In the City, with my father. He used to be a fisherman, many years ago. Now they have machines that do a better job."

She stopped, as her eyes looked past him, scanning the immediate strip of beach ahead of them. It was as if their conversation was not important, but rather something to fill in the idle moments of her mission. But she must have noticed Link's disappointment with this, because she seemed to catch herself up in this action and return her gaze to Link. He too felt the change and he hoped that she possessed some magical, mystical talent that would tell her that Link needed to talk. He wanted her to know that he was so terribly alone in a world that he did not like.

"What about you?" she said gently. "Are you from this area too?"

He tensed unconsciously, although he appreciated her interest in him. She was staring at him and he was captivated by the almost bottomless depths of her eyes. There was a pause before he answered. "Oh, no, not really . . . the installation, back up that way." He pointed toward the direction from which he had come. "I'm . . . staying there for a while."

"I thought so," she said nodding. Her voice was still as soft as the gentle roll of the surf. "I recognized the emblem on your jumpsuit."

He was not surprised by her perceptiveness; yet it made him wonder if she knew what he was. Or rather, what he *had been*. He was sure that she would think it a most unnatural existence. The thought was unsettling, and Link cast it from his mind.

They walked farther. The moon was higher, and it no longer cut a yellow swath across the sea's emerald surface. Link grew more captivated by her, by her warmth that he so dearly needed. Words rattled through his mind, but he could not say them. He felt the conflicts rising up inside his head; he was becoming confused.

Then there came a roaring in his ears that he knew did not come from the sea around him. It grew until it was a scream that echoed down the corridors of space and time, and Link knew that she could not hear it. The moon fell. The sea swam in mind-darkness and the wind became the hot breath of alien stars. His mouth filled with the salty taste of stars' blood.

He faltered, staggering away from her.

"Are you all right?" Her voice slipped gently between the layers of madness.

Pressing his hands to his temples, he turned away. "No." He almost shouted the word. "No . . . it's nothing. I'm okay." Memories and sensations from another time raged

through him. There was a curtain of darkness
enveloping him. He wanted to avoid her; he
did not want her to see him during the attack. "I've got to go now . . ." he heard a
strange voice saying. *Was it his own?* He
could no longer be positive, as he battled to
keep control. Images flickered past his eyes:
warps, pulsars, coronas, and a thousand more
all at once. Link watched them with fear and
fascination as he floated in a netherworld of
delusion.

He was walking. Alone. It was still night,
and he was walking back along the beach
toward the installation. Each step brought
him more firmly into focus, closer to the immense concrete cube. Looking up, he saw it
rising up out of the fog of his conscious
mind, and the thought struck him that he had
returned to it as if by instinct. The attack
had subsided, and it was leaving him. He re-
focused his vision, heard the hushed crashes
of the surf, felt the wet firmness of the sand
beneath his boots.

Exhaling long and slowly, he stopped in
that twilight area between the sea and the
land. He remembered her and turned away
from the dark cube on the cliffs, searching,
hoping . . .

But she was gone.

He was lost; yet he was not. He felt pain;
yet he did not. He feared something, but he
did not want to articulate that fear. The taste
of it was so bitter, and he welcomed it. He
hoped that it was the herald of something
new awakening within himself.

Link inhaled deeply, drawing the sea-strangled air into his body. The salty breath, which once carried the seeds of life itself, rushed into him. He stood silent for a moment, trying to capture the earlier events of the night. But the wind was growing chilly, and finally, he pulled up his collar against it and returned to the installation.

He awoke to a montage of white and green: more tests: wires, screens, charts, words, hands, theories. Everything flowed into one and he accepted it like a purging bath. Link could now wait patiently for the chance to tell Herson what had happened on the beach.

And when he had told the doctor of the entire encounter, Herson sat quietly, stroking his beard. Link watched the man's eyes: small, but expressing concern and intelligence.

"You sound like you enjoyed the experience," said Herson after a long moment of silence.

"Yes, I did . . . I think I did."

"Even though you suffered another deprivation lapse? Immediately afterward?" Herson leaned closer in his chair, staring intently into Link's eyes.

"Yes. I don't think the two events were related. Not really."

"Why not?"

"I just don't." Link raised his voice slightly. "Because, well, there were some other things . . . thoughts I had after I recovered."

"Can you explain these thoughts?"

"I don't know," said Link, looking away, rubbing his eyes out of habit. "Maybe. Before I came back last night, but after the attack, I spent some time just watching the ocean. Alone. It was funny, but it looked *different*. It was like . . . well, I'm not sure . . ."

"This is interesting," said Herson. "Would you like me to supply the analogy?"

"What?"

"Would you like me to try and complete your impression of what it was like? I think I have a good idea as to what it was." Herson smiled.

"How could you?" Link's curiosity was piqued.

"Just a hunch, that's all." Herson grinned.

"All right. Go on, try."

"When you looked out at the ocean after the attack and the meeting with the girl, you felt the same . . . satisfaction, shall we call it? . . . that you enjoyed when you were a cyborg aboard the ship. That's it, isn't it?"

"Yes. I guess it was," said Link, nodding slowly, and admitting the fact to himself for the first time.

"So," said Herson, patting him on the knee. "You see now that it can happen here? On Earth, I mean."

Link nodded.

"That's good," said Herson, as he stood and prepared to leave. "We have at last reached the beginning."

Link started to speak, to question the doctor, but he cut him off: "That's enough for today. Get some rest. I'll see you again to-morrow."

After Herson had left, Link reviewed the last fragments of their conversation, sifting through the words, looking for some grain of insight that might spark off the proper connections in his mind. He knew that Herson seemed to have understood what he had tried to say.

At dusk, Link left the white room and the green robes and the stark corridors of the installation, preferring the cool-blue arms of evening that waited to embrace him. He was drawn to the beach and the tide that was now receding from it. The sky was terribly clear and the sea was smooth, but he sensed an odd mood in the air. As if sudden changes could burst upon the shore with little notice. Already, the retreating tide had speckled the sand with several dead and dying creatures from the sea.

But this time as Link viewed the sight, he was not reminded of life's futility. She had shown him a different view—a new way of seeing in the twilight. It was a place of multiple realities, of this he was now certain. Even in the midst of dying, there could be purpose. He began walking, and continued for almost an hour. He was only vaguely aware of the path of footprints he left in the sand.

Instead, he searched for hers.

The moon grew high and small, becoming lost on the now clouded vault above him. The wind grew stronger and less comforting, less inviting; yet he walked on. But he saw no trace of her. With a growing anxiety, he remembered her words: *There are so many beaches ... so many nights.* Perhaps she was not coming here again? Perhaps he had never seen her in the first place. It was a staggering thought to think that she had only been a bizarre manifestation of his madness.

But no. There was something magical about this place where he walked, where he searched. He would not give up so easily. He knew that where he now walked was a place where a solitary human being had passed nightly to battle death. Link now realized also that there were, perhaps, different kinds of death. Finding her would confirm his feelings.

He rounded a jutting point of land, and he saw her.

Beyond a finger of rocks stretching out to touch the waves stood the girl. As he began walking quickly toward her, he twice saw her pause to return some hapless thing back to the sea.

Then Link slowed his pace, calming himself, suppressing the joy he felt at finding her. He cast a glance downward at the sand and muck that slid past his boots, and he saw something. In the swirling foam, there was a small and slimy thing. Its pores were glutted with sand, suffocating it in the night breeze. Link stooped down and picked it up, feeling its tiny spicules against his palm.

He continued to approach her, and she turned, sensing his nearness, to watch him draw closer. Her eyes dropped to the creature he held in his hand, and she nodded gently.

"I'm sorry," Link said when he was close to her. "About last night. I really don't remember—"

She silenced him with a simple gesture—a lowering of her eyes and a slight shake of her head.

"I'm sorry," he said again. Then after a pause: "I've come to . . . join you."

She smiled and her eyes danced with lively amber and brown. As Link watched her, he felt a smile forming on his own lips—the first in a long, long time, it seemed. She laughed softly and looked out to the star-filled sea.

Pulling back his arm, Link flung the creature far out into the night. Time seemed to slow as he watched the thing's path describe a graceful arc across the violet sky. Masked by the whisper of the surf, it noiselessly penetrated the surface and was gone.

Seeing this, Link felt an atavistic surge within his mind. It was not unlike the cybernetic taste of the stars themselves. Something inside himself was coming to life again.

"It's beautiful, isn't it?" she asked, as if she could sense the feelings in his soul.

Link turned to her and nodded. He reached out to touch her hand.

"Your name," he said softly. "What is it?"

Caring for its inhabitants is only one function of the City. It must also care for itself. The steps it must take, if it is to survive, must inevitably begin. Slowly at first, but efficiently performed and irresistibly final.

TWO

"Go, the Mass is ended," said Father Patrilli as he faced the almost empty interior of the church. He closed his outstretched arms, bringing his palms together, lowering his head to listen to the isolated sounds of rustling feet, nervous coughs, and whispered prayers. The small group of attendees made their way to the crowded avenues of the City.

The altar boy was looking up at him, and Patrilli took notice with an air of resignation on his face. "All right, go on. Let's get out of here."

The young boy got off his knees quickly and led the way to the sacristy to the right of the altar. As they exited, Patrilli looked out at the last of the gray heads, the stooped gaits, the wrinkled faces. They were all relics from an earlier age, like Patrilli himself.

Shaking his head sadly, the priest left the altar to be touched by the shadowy gloom of the chamber off the church's nave. The altar boy had already peeled off his black cassock and was hanging it in an old cedar armoire.

"See you next week, Father," said the boy, after he blew out the candles and put away the small glass tray holding the cruets of wine and water.

"Yes, next Sunday. Goodbye, then." Patrilli raised a hand to wave to the boy, but he had already disappeared beyond the old oak door which led to the sidewalk.

Slowly, the old priest removed his vestments—all expensively woven silks and satins, carefully brocaded and hand-stitched—and placed them on wooden hangers. He had been repeating this ritual for almost forty years, but for some reason that morning he recalled with a great vividness the first time he had donned the vestments to celebrate his first Mass. It had been the day of his graduation from the seminary and he had been so deliriously happy, so proud! His parents had been seated in the first row of their town's small quarry-stone and mortar church, and he remembered how his hands trembled the first time he took up the Eucharist from the golden chalice, held it up before the congregation while the joyous peal of the communion bells filled his ears, and proclaimed it to be the body of the Savior. He could still see the image of his father kneeling at the rail, eyes closed, white pasty tongue extended, awaiting the first Host from his chalice.

Patrilli shook his head and wiped at moisture in the corners of his eyes. The image faded and died. It was odd, though, how the *past* was becoming clearer to him than the present, how he was having moments when it was very difficult to concentrate on things that were happening around him. In a clear flash of insight, one part of his mind told the rest that that day in a small Maryland church was a long time dead; there was no going back to it.

Locking the door behind him, he crossed the well-tended lawns past a single dogwood tree and up the back steps to the rectory, where Mrs. Krauch, his housekeeper, had breakfast cooking.

"Good morning, Father," she said as she poked and stirred at the pans on the old electric stove. "Have a good crowd this morning?"

"What? Oh . . . no, not really. Less than usual maybe, I don't know."

"Well, don't let it get you down. I've got some real bacon for us this morning. Ain't that a treat?"

Patrilli nodded and forced a smile to his face as he pulled up a chair. The aroma of the frying bacon was, indeed, a pleasant sensation, and for a moment he was twelve years old again and he was seated at the small table in Mother's kitchen and she was fixing him breakfast before seeing him off to school. He lifted a glass of grapefruit juice to his lips and the bracing chill of it smacked him back to the present. He was disappointed at this.

"There was a call for you while you was at Mass, Father. I almost forgot." Mrs. Krauch swept to the table with a steaming plate of scrambled eggs and several strips of glistening bacon. "Toast'll be ready in a minute."

Patrilli looked up at the spindly, wrinkled woman. "A call?"

"Yes, Father. Someone from the City government. Some Office or another, I didn't catch the name, he said it so fast."

"What did he want?" Patrilli speared a piece of bacon with his fork.

"He didn't say. Said he would be stopping by to see you after two."

"Today? Doesn't he know it's Sunday?"

"Now, come on now, Father. You know that don't matter much to people anymore." She placed two slices of hot buttered toast beside his plate.

Patrilli stared off into space, wishing that he was back in that warm, bright, old-fashioned kitchen of fifty years ago. He paused, looked at the gray-haired old woman. "No, I suppose you're right, Mrs. Krauch. I suppose you're right."

He finished the breakfast in silence as his housekeeper whisked about the kitchen, rubbing and polishing, scrubbing and rinsing. She seemed to have a secret tap on an infinite energy supply. She was always light and cheerful, always wanting to help, to renew, to make right. She was probably older than Patrilli, obviously born too early to take benefit of the gerontological Treatments, and apparently none the worse for it.

Leaving his dishes on the counter top, he left the woman to her tasks and ascended the stairs to his study on the second floor. Without thinking about it, he automatically punched in a newsfax request on his desk-top terminal. As the unit hummed into action, he realized what he had done, and it distressed him. He was doing that sort of thing more and more lately: drifting away from the *now* of his thoughts and even his actions, discovering what he was doing as if he was a spectator to his own life sometimes. That these things suggested senility or perhaps even a growing madness was an unpleasant thought and he immediately banished it from his mind, concentrating on the sheets that were already dropping into the in-basket. How he missed *real* newspapers! He remembered the *Tribune* with its colorful front pages, its distinctive logo and graphics, its flamboyant editorials and columns. Now that everything was dispensed on the featureless print-outs, the news was different, cold, distant. And the cost, he thought painfully, was so much more than back then. Even the terminal—a necessity in such an age of complexity—was a luxury to his church. The loss of parish revenues had long ago forced the archdiocese to subsidize the churches, and the budget had been stripped clean. It had been many years since Patrilli even bothered to pass a collection plate during Mass.

Ignoring the newsfax, which was completing its run, Patrilli turned to his desk, where an unfinished letter to Father Moynihan lay upon the blotter. Remembering it only vaguely, he picked it up and read what he had written the night before:

Dear Michael:

I am sorry it has taken me so long to answer your last letter. I know it would be so much easier to use the phones, but letters have always been

*more comfortable for me—I can col-
lect my thoughts, organize them, and
get them down so much better with a
pen. It is not that I have been busy.
Quite the contrary. There is so little
to do any longer.*

*I share your concern about the loss
of parishioners, although things at
your parish do not seem as bad as here.
There is something about this city, all
cities probably, that works against us,
I think. Nothing permanent anymore. Change always. No one seems to
have anything even bordering on a
tradition. Everything is dispensable:
buildings, ideas, people. I often feel
that I am ill-suited for this world,
and I wonder why the Lord has allowed me to live to see its coming.*

But that is not the worst of things.

*You remember my mentioning in
the last letter about loss of faith? If
anything, the situation has worsened.
I have almost forgotten what it is like
to have a peaceful night's sleep. It's as
if I have reached a stage now where
the thoughts leave me numb, detached,
disinterested. As if I no longer care.
My mind seems to be not much with
the present, and I find myself getting
lost in memories more and more.*

Michael, do you remember our days in the seminary? When you would keep me up at night with your questions about theology? When you asked me what I thought it would be like to finally stand face-to-face with the Creator? Well, there are times when I feel like we talked like that only yesterday, and I want to cry out to you, Michael, that maybe we have already met our Creator, and it is not the Lord, but ourselves. I don't wish to believe that this world is part of any Divine Plan. The scientists say that there are millions of worlds out there like our own. Could ours be of any special importance, then? And what of the creatures they've found floating like zeppelins in the gases of Jupiter? What do they know of Original Sin? Of Satan? Of Christ?

My faith is like our Church, like a cliff of flaking shale that is constantly giving way to the erosion of the waves striking it. To give ground is to be the lesser for it. And now, at times when I seem to be most lucid, most honest with myself (and honest with you), I think that maybe my mind is also like that fragile cliff.

At those times, I am forced to look upon the pieces of my life. The church within which I work, in this titan-City, is like a museum, and I am

but its curator. My life an artifact, a
relic, only fit for such a place. Down
all the years, Michael, and I should be
content. But I am obviously not.

There are times when I even think
that I might

The letter had ended at that point, and Patrilli replaced the sheet to the desk with a trembling hand. He had difficulty remembering
parts of the letter, but he *did* know what he
might have written had he not lost his nerve.

That he might what? he asked himself, already knowing the answer. He shuddered as
he recalled the moments when he would seem
to drift off into a misty world of half vision
where he calmly checked off the possible
ways of killing himself. He knew that it was
the ultimate rejection of God, of self, and of
any chance to know the Divine. It was a
horror, an unthinkable sin, yet he had not
only thought of it, he had dwelled on it.

But it could not end like that. He would
not allow it. He would never be so weak.

Looking back to the desk, Patrilli felt a
wave of strength pass over him. He was en-
joying a spell of clear thinking at that moment
and he allowed himself a smile. Warm sunlight
spotlighted the dancing dust motes at his window and he felt reassured that he was once
again aware of such simple yet beautiful
things. He would finish the letter to Father
Moynihan, knowing that he must be honest
with his friend and himself. He knew that it

was not so important that he finish the letter just for its own sake, although he was so inclined, or even that his friend should know his most troubling, darkest thoughts. Rather, it was the confessional aspect of the communication that was most meaningful. Patrilli understood the psychology of the Sacraments only too well.

Picking up the pen, he wrote:

> *be the agent of my own death. In clearer times—such as this present one—I know this will never happen, and I wonder if the thought is as binding as the deed. I pray that it is not.*
>
> *Later today, I must meet with a representative from Chicago. And although I do not know the nature of the meeting, I am sure that it is nothing beneficial. There are few good things in this place, Michael.*
>
> *I await word from you and pray that you remain healthy and at peace.*
>
> *Yours in Christ,*
>
> *Joseph*

Patrilli picked up the sheet and slipped it into the slot of the desk terminal. Instantly an optical-scanner began transforming his words into impulses that would be sped across the continent to the other priest's terminal.

Once the letter was dispatched, Patrilli was filled with an instant of dread, a sense of loss and non-direction, as if now there would be nothing to do with his time. He looked at the basket of newsfax sheets and dismissed it. No, he did not want to know what was happening in the world. It was always full of unpleasantness. He thought of his films—his one luxury, a room crammed with cans of ancient prints of films from the twentieth century. He had been an eager student of cinema when he was young, so many years ago, and dreamed then of becoming a "film maker," a term very much in vogue at the time. He had worked at developing his craft, but never got the break, the recognition needed to become truly accomplished. He sought comfort in becoming a collector of old films, a pastime that had persisted even after he had entered the seminary, and which he continued throughout his life. Yes, he would get out the old Bell & Howell, select something light—a Woody Allen, perhaps—and get lost in the flickering images.

Looking at his watch, he knew that this could not be. It was too late to begin a film; the man from the City would be coming soon. Odd that he had not noticed the passage of time while engrossed in his letter, in his rambling thoughts. And so he sat, silent and utterly passive, recalling great and memorable scenes from his collection. There was one in particular that haunted him, especially now. It was from a German film called *Metropo-*

lis; Patrilli shuddered as his mind's eye conjured up Lang's great machine, a generator of some sort, upon which a battery of men slaved in precise, machine-like movements. Patrilli remembered how the image of the enormous, pyloned thing slowly changed into the likeness of a beast from the Pit, from the depths of horror and despair. The stark image, the surreal metaphor, was so apt, he thought, so full of vision. He shook his head, knowing that Chicago had far surpassed both the majesty and the decadence of that German dream-city.

There was a tap on the door, and a familiar voice. "Excuse me, Father, but there's someone here to see you."

"All right," he called out. "Thanks, Mrs. Krauch. Tell him I'll be right down."

He heard her footsteps on the stairs softly receding and he rose to follow her. Pausing before an ornately framed mirror, he regarded the face within the oval, ran his fingers through his wispy gray hair. His blue eyes reflected a sadness.

Downstairs, Mrs. Krauch had seated the visitor in the front-room office—a little-used room that had once been the scene of thousands of counseling sessions for members of the church. But no one ever came for Patrilli's advice anymore. Patrilli entered to greet a man of perhaps forty, although it was now impossible to determine a person's real age. The man stood up; he was quite tall, had curly hair, greenish eyes, a large nose, and a mouth that seemed naturally to reflect some sort of pain.

"Good afternoon, Father. My name is Kuczek. I'm with the Department of Census and Demography."

Patrilli took the offered hand and grasped it lightly as he spoke. "Good day, Mr. Kuczek. What can I do for you?"

"Not much, except listen to what I have to say. Could we sit down, please?"

Patrilli nodded, seated himself behind a barren desk, and directed Kuczek to a chair in front. "All right. What do you want to tell me?"

"Chicago's a big city, Father. Twenty-five million as of the last census in January. According to our records of that date, less than two hundred fifty thousand citizens reported any religious affiliations. That's a terribly small percentage of the total population. Out of that number, there's maybe seventy thousand Catholics . . ."

The man's face radiated a negativeness that was quite plain, although his voice remained inflectionless, precise, unfeeling. Patrilli knew what the figures meant; he had experienced them on a personal level.

"I'm surprised that there's *that* many," said the priest.

Kuczek seemed to miss the sardonic overtones of Patrilli's words and continued. "Yes, well, at any rate, my department has conducted a study which indicates that the City has allocated far too much structure-space to Worship Centers such as your church." The man paused for a moment and searched through a shoulder bag which he held upon his lap. Then he produced a thick sheaf of computer-printed documents. As he quickly fanned through the pages, Patrilli caught glimpses of many charts and graphs in bold black ink. "And so, a practical solution to this problem was devised, and approved by the directors of the department. You may find all the details in this copy which I can leave with you, if you promise to return it to the department."

Patrilli eyed the manuscript contemptuously. "I'm afraid my eyes aren't as good as they used to be. Do you think you could just give me a summary?"

"Oh, I fully intend to, Father. I'm afraid that you'll have to give up this church. Demography has found that the Catholic population density for the Sector doesn't warrant the number of existing churches. We're reducing that number to a more applicable amount. Your church is one of the ones that is no longer deemed necessary."

No longer deemed, thought Patrilli. *The bastards. The cold, insensitive bastards.* Something lurched deep within him and he felt a change overtaking him. Anger? Resignation? Hysteria? He did not know, suddenly did not care. "What does the archdiocese have to say about this?" he heard himself ask, as if another part of himself had decided to carry on a civil conversation, a front.

"Let me see ... oh, yes, Cardinal Richter, that's his name. He was notified of our findings and although he was reluctant to transfer deed of the church property, he was persuaded to see the sense of the entire project." Kuczek smiled wanly.

Patrilli felt his throat grow thick and his mouth was full of cotton. "What will I do then? Where will I go?"

"We don't have any say over such things, Father. I would assume that one of your bishops will take care of that, don't you think?"

"Yes . . . one of our bishops, yes."

"Very well, then, our computers will be drawing up the new directives for the future use of this structure-space and new assignments will be coming out in a day or two. There will be some forms to fill out for our records and arrangements made for the transfer of your possessions. We will be in touch about that via the terminals. But the department thought that it would be best if we contacted you personally about this matter first."

"That's very thoughtful of you," said Patrilli.

"Why, thank you, Father."

He was rubbing his temples, closing his eyes, shutting out the image of the hateful Kuczek. The reality of the man's words now breaking through the barriers. *Is this the way it will end? Is this the way?* The thought resounded in his head.

"I suppose that will be all for now, Father. I certainly hope that this decision will not inconvenience you too much. It's a big country, though. Still plenty of work for people like you to do. I wouldn't worry if I were you. And I'm sure you understand our position. The City of Chicago cannot stand still. Times change and we must change with them." Kuczek stood and gathered up his shoulder bag, extending his right hand to the priest. "Good luck and goodbye."

Patrilli arose and limply shook the man's hand, but said nothing. He wondered if his face communicated his troubled, ambivalent feelings, even though it was doubtful that Kuczek would be aware of them, be able to interpret them. He showed the man to the door, closed it slowly behind him. It was as if he was closing a door on his own life at the same time. Wretched as it had become, it was all he had left.

And now they would take even that away from him.

Time became a featureless, shapeless mist through which he drifted without consideration of it. He spoke little to Mrs. Krauch other than saying something vague about the church being renovated soon and that she would not be needed for a while. He spent most of the hours walking aimlessly from room to room thinking of nothing, or practically nothing. Then there were moments when he would stop himself, catching himself in the midst of a nonsense thought, and be sharply aware of his surroundings, of his actions, and begin to ponder what indeed he was doing in a particular room, at a particular hour. He slept little if any, although he maintained the ritual of undressing and lying in the darkness of his bedroom.

Several days must have passed before his desk terminal clacked into life and deposited a yellow coded-urgent fax in the basket. Patrilli was standing by the window, looking

out across the small parish lawn at the alumi-
num-white towers of the City in the distance,
when the message came through. Picking it
up he read the top page, which was like an
abstract of what was contained within the
following pages:

> JØSEPH PATRILLI
> CCSSN 513-87-2338-90-G
> CITY SECTØR 19-Bv7
> TERMINAL 3896556008
> ØCCUPANCY ØF STRUCTURE-SPACE
> 19-bv7/520037
> [GENERIC: ØUR LADY ØF FATIMA
> CHURCH (CATHØLIC)]
> TERMINATIØN 12:00/08/12/81

Flipping absently through the remaining
pages, he saw many forms which were
riddled with warnings and instructions, and
blank spaces that must be filled in and signed
and dated. It was a feeble monument to the
bureaucratic regimen that had overtaken humanity. A piece of cheap paper, and yet it
was also something of ultimate power and authority. Patrilli threw the sheets upon the
desk, picked up a pen, and began to write,
but not to the city.

Dear Michael,

*I must write you again, even
though you have not yet replied to my
last letter. They are taking away my
church within a few days, Michael.
They are taking it away from me.*

Richter knows, and apparently does not care. I have lost track of time, I am feeling ill, and do not know what I will do from minute to minute. I have missed saying the morning Mass for at least several days.

I have done little else but to sit in this room and contemplate my life—its past and its future. My present is so empty, I try not to think about it.

Dismissing Mrs. Krauch was most difficult, and although I am not sure, I think I lied to her, telling her that the church was being remodeled and that she could take a vacation of sorts.

The City has sent me forms to fill out and return. I have ignored them, destroyed, lost them . . . I cannot remember which. Bishop Weinstein sent me a directive ordering me to St. Louis to work in a hospital. Good work, I suppose, but I do not want to go there. I feel that I must demonstrate in some way what these monsters here have done to me. I only hope that I am capable of hurting them as much as they have hurt me.

Goodbye, my friend. I do not know when I will again be in touch, or even if I will ever see you again. But I must confess one last thing: I want to feel

righteous, as if I were doing something
for Christ, but I know deep down that
I am doing it for myself.

In pacem,

Joseph

The hours passed like the featureless waters
of a roaring stream, and he paid them little
attention. With no one in the large rectory
to prepare his meals, he ate little, rummaging
in the kitchen for an occasional piece of
cheese, some bread perhaps. He was interrupted from his growing reveries once by the
desk terminal, which issued a warning from
some government agency that he was in vio-
lation of some such code, and that he must respond immediately to the series of forms
needed to make his transfer "official."

Calmly he reposed himself at the terminal
and typed out a short message:

GØ FUCK YØURSELF

and laughed hysterically as the machine duti-
fully sent off the reply to the City's computer
centers, where some shocked civil servant, he
imagined, would soon be reading it.

Later that afternoon, he sat with the Bell &
Howell, creaking and whirring behind his
right ear, watching a scratchy print of an old
film called *Dr. Strangelove*. It was an
uproariously funny film and it seemed to re-

inforce the message he had dispatched to the City.

While he sat watching the swept-wing bomber skimming nightmarishly close to the Asian steppes, the desk terminal clacked another message and left a single page in the basket. Later, when he picked it up to read it, he was only vaguely aware of the words, which seemed to say something about facing legal action and a visit from the police. There was a time when such a message would have set off alarms throughout his system and he would have reacted to the idea of being arrested with cold fear. But now, he simply laid the fax on his desk and returned to the task of rewinding his precious reels and placing them carefully within the scarred, battered tins.

Later that evening, Patrilli sat in the darkened kitchen, nibbling on a piece of cold bread. There was a faint glow at the window, the last remnants of sunset, and shadows crept slowly across the room like predatory beasts. Patrilli sat at the table, not tasting food, only half-seeing in the spectral light.

There was a knock at the door. Authoritative. Confident and loud.

Standing and walking absently to the door, Patrilli opened it to see the one he expected, thinking that it was fitting that they should come at night. Pogroms were always more dramatic in the dark hours. There was a solitary officer standing on the colonnaded porch. He wore a tightly fitting uniform of the traditional blue with white trim, a helmet that looked like a pearlescent egg with an amberglass visor across the eyes. There was a menacing-looking sidearm on his belt. Patrilli was unable to see the man's face.

"You Joseph Patrilli?"

"That's right."

"I have a warrant from C and D. Says you've failed to reply to directives on a relocation."

"That's right."

"Look, uh . . . Father, you're supposed to be transferred from this property as of this evening. And I'm here to see that you do."

"Yes, I know that, Officer. Would you care to step inside for a moment?" Patrilli stood back and ushered the man through the foyer and closed the door behind. He felt strangely light-headed; he was very much aware of his blood pounding behind his ears. "I'm afraid I haven't prepared to move yet, as you can see."

"You're going to have to get moving. This isn't good. You not being ready like this."

"I'm sorry, Officer. It's going to be quite an adjustment for me. I've lived here for many years, you know."

"That's what they all say," said the officer, as he flipped up his visor and slowly removed the helmet.

Patrilli studied the man's face. He was young, very young. A wild shock of blond hair, eyebrows so blond they were almost white, bright eyes like polished blue stones, tanned shimmering complexion, and an expression that radiated a certain rawness.

"I'm going to have to arrest you," the officer continued. "Your possessions will be collected and placed in storage, and—" The policeman paused, looking past Patrilli's face, upward toward the far wall. "What's that?" He raised a gloved hand, pointing.

Turning, Patrilli saw the object of the man's attention. It was a large crucifix, made of hewn, heavy oak, with the Corpus made of a burnished bronze. "That's a statue," said the priest. "It depicts the death of Christ."

The officer shook his head, his face reflecting something like disgust.

"What's wrong?" asked Patrilli, feeling himself lapsing into one of his now familiar sequences of disorientation, fogginess.

"That's one of the most horrible-looking things I've ever seen," said the officer. "It's grotesque."

Patrilli regarded the crucifix as if viewing it through a gray mist. The tortured shape of Jesus had always seemed so *right* to him; it had been one of his earliest memories, one of the things in life that one accepts without question. He had never seen it as a singularly horrible thing, smacking of barbarism, insensitivity, grossness. It was as if the officer had torn a veil away from Patrilli's face, allowing him to see clearly for the first time in his life. Suddenly he felt very small and foolish; as if he had been stripped naked before the officer. There was a part of him that wanted to defend the blasphemy, to explain that the image of the Savior on the cross represented the most important moment in the history of man; however, another part would have nothing of that. That other self, that other mind, saw the folly in that, simply because it felt that perhaps the officer had been correct. *What's happening to me?* He felt himself losing control, like a ship being tossed capriciously in a storm. Struggling against the two tides of contradictory thought, he clenched his fists and stared helplessly at the officer, who did not seem to take notice of the priest's growing tension.

"You're going to have to come with me now," the officer was saying.

"No! I won't!" he cried suddenly, surprised at his own words, as if they were not his own. "*You* talk about ugliness . . . you bastard. You're no better than the pigs who put the Jews to the ovens!"

"What? What're you talking about?"

Patrilli moved from behind the desk and shook his fist in the officer's face. The priest's lips were curled back into a tormented rictus, teeth clenched together, the muscles in his jaws quivering like tautly stretched cords.

"There've been others like you," he said, as if each word was an affront. "They tried to exterminate a whole race of people. Brilliant people! Doctors, scientists, artists, all of them gassed and burned in ovens like coal!" He paused and looked at the officer, his eyes glassing over, seeing yet not seeing. "They used their skin to make wallets and lampshades. Their ashes for soap."

"That's ridiculous," said the officer, reaching for a small object on his belt. It was a radio. Turning half away from Patrilli, the officer pressed a digital key and spoke: "Western, this is Unit 377. I'm at Sector

19-Bv7. I think you better notify the clinic, I'm gonna have to bring the subject over there."

As the radio squawked a seemingly unintelligible reply, Patrilli turned quickly, spying the large crucifix on the wall behind the officer. It was as if he were a spectator to his own action as he reached for the heavy object, grasping it with both hands knuckled whitely about Christ's legs. Anger rushed up through him like a thick column of bile, choking him, cutting off all sense of control. The hate he suddenly felt charged him like electricity as he brought the crucifix over his head and swung it like an ax.

". . . yeah, right," the officer was saying into the radio, "I think he's going a little wacko on me. I'll check back in when—"

The sentence died upon his lips, cut short by the left arm and bar of the cross as Patrilli drove it savagely into the back of the officer's skull. The priest watched the uniformed man crumple to the floor, landing on his back, a dark stain quickly forming on the carpet beneath his head. Unseeing eyes stared up at Patrilli and in that instant, he felt the hate, the fear, the rage flee him like a banished demon. His breath came in hurried gasps, he felt himself choking as his throat became thick, his mouth dry.

The radio lay on the floor by the still body. It suddenly began to squawk and bleat in a language of static and jargon. Bending down, Patrilli picked it up, studied it for a moment, switched it off.

He was extremely light-headed, his limbs still trembled from the surge of adrenaline, his heart fluttered dangerously. Sitting down behind the desk, he buried his face in his hands, and awaited the sound of *them* at the door.

He was taken to a clinic for examination, and later shuttled to a rehabilitation center. It was there, he knew, during his more lucid moments, that they would begin a series of "reconditioning" sessions. He was still recovering from the beating he had received when arrested, and there were fleeting scraps of memories of something heavy slashing through his intestines, something heavier striking his jaw, his breath escaping him like air from a crushed bellows. He could still remember the blackness engulfing him and his thought that he never imagined it would be so easy to die.

But they did not let him die.

And so he lay in his cell, in a bed, writing a final letter to Moynihan. There was something within that did not want to forget, that did not want the record wiped so totally clean. Perhaps he could find a sympathetic nurse who would transmit the message.

The letter rambled on, reflecting the state of Patrilli's tormented soul, his unseamed mind, but he did manage to reconstruct the deed which undid him. He closed with the following observations, which displayed a rare moment of insight, and served as a fitting touchstone to his life:

... *and I know that this City cannot punish me severely enough. It lacks the inclination, the understanding, to make the punishment fit the crime. The crime was growing old. Their punishment was not only to take away my church, but also my guilt.*

I am just a flashing ember in a purging fire. But I fear for the rest of you, Michael. If they can take away your guilt, your most private means of punishing yourselves, what will be left of your humanity?

The answer lies in our future like a dark, rough beast, and I am at least thankful that I will not live to greet its spectral face.

Pax vobiscum,

Joseph

*Time passes and new solutions are
applied to the old problems.
Perspectives change through time.
Priorities are reordered. Values
are reassessed. The men of the City,
working in concert with their great
machines, slowly redefine their relationship with the City, and sadly,
themselves.*

THREE

Signals chimed throughout the great City of Chicago as another work shift prepared to begin their service to the urban complex.

Benjamin Cipriano sat down at his console, casting a quick glance outward to the Breeder Tank below him. He switched his attention to the controls and opened up a communications channel to the Tank. He pulled the psi-helmet over his head and pressed the throat mike close to his larynx. "Good morning, Feraxya. Feeling okay today?"

His scalp tingled as invisible fingers slipped into his skull to massage his brain. The helmet fed her psi words into him: "Good morning to you, too, Benjamin." The "voice" sounded just vaguely feminine to him, and his imagination reinforced the conceptualization. "I'm feeling fine. Everything is normal. You know I always feel comfortable when you are on the console."

"Thank you," said Cipriano, pausing for a moment. "Now, I have some tests to run this morning, so we'd better get started." He flipped several toggles as he continued speaking to her. "It's all routine stuff . . . blood

sugar, enzyme scans, placental balance quo-
tients . . . things like that. Nothing to worry
about."

There was a short silence before she
touched his mind again: "I never worry
when you're on. Perhaps we'll have time to
talk, later on?"

"If you want to. I'll have some time in a
few minutes. Bye now." He switched off the
communications channel and stared at the
protoplasmic nightmare on the other side of
his console-booth window. Stretched out before him were all the Breeder Tanks for his
Sector of the City. They were Chicago's
symbols of deliverance from misery and deprivation for all the City's members. Except,
perhaps, the Host-Mothers themselves. Cipriano wondered about them in general, Feraxya
in particular, and what their lives must be
like.

Technically, Feraxya was human. Visually,
however, she was an amorphous, slithering,
amoeba-like thing. She was tons of genetically cultured flesh, a human body in-
flated and stretched and distended until it
was many times its normal size. Lost beneath
her abundant flesh was a vestigial skeleton
which floated disconnected and unmoving in
a gelatinous sea. Her bioneered organs were
swollen to immense proportions and hundreds
of liters of blood pumped through her extensive circulatory system.

Yet he knew, even as he activated the
probes that plunged into her soft flesh, that
she was still a woman to him. A very special
kind of woman. From her earliest moments of

consciousness, she had spent her life contained within the glassteel walls of the Breeder Tank. It was an immense cube, ten meters on each side, the back wall covered with connecting cables and tubes which carried her life-support systems, monitoring devices, and bio-medical elements that were necessary for her continued maintenance.

To Cipriano, she *was* the glassteel cube. Feraxya had no face, no arms, no legs; all those things were buried beneath the folds of swollen flesh that rippled with life-fluids. And yet she was a person, a Citizen of Chicago, who had received the standard education by means of special input programs piped through her sensory nerves and into her brain, bypassing her useless eyes and ears. She also represented several basic changes from previous Host-Mothers. Feraxya was a third-generation mutant; careful genetic selection and programming had given her primary-level psi powers, which were used in communication and eventually for education. Chicago's Central Computers postulated that the quiet, undisturbed environ of the Breeder Tank would be an ideal atmosphere for the development of psi.

Ben looked away from the giant tank, leaned back in his chair, and watched the monitoring data come clicking into the tapes at his console. As he waited for the data to accumulate, his gaze wandered down the long row of other consoles like his own, where many other Breeder Tank Monitors sat reading their indicators and print-outs. Each Monitor was charged with his own Host-

Mother; each Host-Mother held within her an enlarged uterus that was filled with thirty human fetuses.

It was in this way that the Host-Mothers provided the City with every desired type of Citizen. There were no outcasts, no misfits, now that society was shaped by the benevolent but highly efficient Central Computers of Chicago. An entire hierarchy was cybernetically conceived and programmed, then handed down through the bureaucratic chain until it reached the Bioneers and Eugenicists. In Chicago's massive Eugenic Complex, hundreds of Host-Mothers like Feraxya carried the fetuses of the next generation of Citizens. Laborers, artists, scientists, bureaucrats, and technicians—all pre-coded and expected.

A message suddenly flashed on Cipriano's console which reminded him to check the night-shift Monitor's report. He did this thing and found it satisfactory. Feraxya had only recently received her first uterine implant and there was little for him to do at this point except routine systems-checks. Later when her brood of fetuses grew and began to crowd her great womb, Cipriano's tasks would also grow. A Host-Mother nearing the end of gestation required much attention.

He replaced the psi-helmet to his head and signaled to her. A tingling sensation touched his mind as she was raised from her inner thoughts: "Yes, Ben?"

"The databanks were still filling," he said. "I've got some free time. Thought you might want to talk for a little while."

"Yes, I would. Thank you. I wanted to tell you about the dream I had . . ."

"A dream?" he asked. "About what?"

"About you. I think about you a lot."

"I didn't know that," said Ben, smiling self-consciously. His words were only a half-truth.

"Yes, it's true . . ." She paused and his mind leapt at the emptiness she created there. "Ben?" she began again.

"Yes?"

"Do you ever think about me? When you're not here, working?"

"Well, yes. I guess I do. Sometimes."

"I'm glad," she said. "You're different from my other Monitors. Of course I'm sleeping most of that time anyway."

"Different?" The word did not sit well in his mind. The Monitors were planned to be quite similar. "How do you mean?"

"You're kinder," she said. "More understanding, I think. It's just easier to talk with you."

"Thank you, Feraxya. I'm just trying to be myself, though."

"Your mate is very lucky to have someone like you," she said candidly. "I guess I should tell you that I've thought about having you myself. Even though I know it's impossible."

Ben paused for a moment, stirred and somewhat shaken by the mental image her suggestion brought to mind. "You could use your Id-Tapes if you really wanted—" He tried to be helpful but she interrupted him.

"That's little more than masturbation."

"I'm sorry," he said. "I was just trying to suggest something that might help, that's all."

"You're sweet. But that's not what I want from you. If I could have it my way it would be like the dream. I had a real body, like you, and we were going through the City at night. It was bright and beautiful. Sometimes I wish it could have been like that."

She paused, and Cipriano searched for any subliminal meaning in her words. There were people who would interpret them as dangerous. He wondered what she meant by them. "It wasn't meant to be," he said finally, shallowly.

"I know. And the Host-Mothers are needed. Someone must serve," she said slowly, as if she were contemplating the implications of what she was saying.

"That's true," he said. "Besides—"

Cipriano was interrupted by the chatter of his console. The results from the morning's test began to flash upon his grid. A large graph appeared and flickered violently; superimposed over the graph was a one-word message: CRITICAL.

"Just a minute, Feraxya," he said, staring at the alarm signal in semi-shock. "Uh ... some of the results have just come in and I've got to check them out. I'll get back to you as soon as I can, okay?"

"All right, Ben. We can talk later."

He threw off the helmet and depressed several digital keys, requesting clarification of the warning signal. Cipriano read through the figures, double-checked them, and started an entire new series of tests to ensure against errors.

As the console began to click and chatter with the new instructions, he called his Superior, Faro Barstowe. Several seconds passed before the man's lean, fox-like face appeared on the screen: "Yes, what is it?"

"Cipriano here. Breeder Tank 0078-D. Generic name: Feraxya. My routine monitoring has picked up what looks like a nucleotide dysfunction. Probable cause is an inadequate enzyme transfer. Too early to tell yet. Just calling to let you know that I'm running a double check."

Barstowe's face seemed tense. "Let's see . . . You've got a litter of thirty. RNA Code 45a7c. Superior Range. Administrator Class. That sound right?"

"Yessir. That's right," said Cipriano, watching the man's small shining eyes burn into him, even through the screen.

"All right, Cipriano. It's been sixty-four days since implantation. That makes it too late for an injection to change or rectify the enzyme transfer. Collect all the data you can from the second scan. I'll call Bioneering and send some men over there to see what's up. That's all for now." The screen blacked out, leaving Ben with the cool sounds of the console.

When he read through the second-test results, he knew that they only confirmed what he had first imagined. There was indeed a dysfunction in Feraxya's system; but he could do nothing until the Bioneers arrived. His first thought was to contact her, so that she would be aware of what was happening inside her great body. But he knew that would not be possible until he received word from Barstowe.

It was several minutes before the white-uniformed specialists from Bioneering entered his booth. One of them read over the data collected from his console while the other two adjusted their white, antiseptic, helmeted suits as they prepared to enter the Breeder Tank Area itself. Cipriano looked past them, through the glass window, to Feraxya, who floated within her prison still ignorant of her own problems.

Later, as he watched the Bioneers scurrying about Feraxya's Tank, he wondered if she could, somehow, sense their nearness, their insensitive prying into the secrets of her grotesque body. He wanted to talk to her, and he entertained the notion of contact as his eyes fell upon the psi-helmet by the console.

One of the Bioneers returned to the booth, quickly removing his helmet and wiping some perspiration from his forehead. He looked at Cipriano and shook his head.

"What's that mean?" said Ben.

"Not good," said the man in white. "There hasn't been any reaction between the DNA/enzyme interface. The 'blueprint injections' didn't copy at all. That's why you were getting the alarms."

"Which means . . . ?" asked Cipriano.

"Which means her fetuses would be completely variable if we brought them to term." The man paused and gestured out toward

Feraxya's Tank. "*Randoms*—that's what we're growing in that one."

"What do we do now?"

"You'd better call Barstowe," said the Bioneer. "My men'll be making an official report, but I think he'd appreciate knowing about it now."

Cipriano knew what Barstowe would say: they would have to remove her brood. He wondered what Feraxya's reaction would be to the decision. Remembering how pleased she had been to receive her first implantation, Cipriano did not look forward to the moment when he would have to confront her with the news.

After he had contacted Barstowe and relayed the results of the Bioneers' inspection, the Superior shook his head, grimacing. "That's too bad. Going to throw us off schedule. I'll arrange for Stander to prepare for a 'scrape' as soon as possible. Tomorrow morning, hopefully."

"I was wondering when I should tell Feraxya about it," said Cipriano.

The fox-like features stared at him for a moment. "You'll have plenty of time in the morning. Don't worry about it. You really don't have anything else to do today, why don't you get out of here?"

"All right," said Cipriano. "But I hope she understands why." Barstowe didn't answer; the screen had already blacked. Ben shook his head slowly and shut down his console. He left the Eugenic Complex and took the Rapids home to his con-apt, hoping that

the following day would be less difficult than
the present one.

That night, Jennifer wanted him.

She was warm and young and fashionably
lean; and he wanted her, too. He always did.
She was something of a romantic, since she
always used candles to illuminate their love-
making, but Cipriano didn't mind.

Jennifer helped him attach the electrodes
to his forehead; she had already hooked herself into the machine. They lay side by side,
naked, in the candlelight as the machine
beneath their bed hummed and touched their
pleasure centers. Physiological feedback was
encoded from each of them, amplified, and
routed into each other as mutual stimuli.
Their orgasms were reached simultaneously
with the aid of the machine. Never touching
each other, not needing to do so, there was no
chance of a non-approved conception. Afterward, they lay in silence, smiling from the
rush of moist satisfaction. Jennifer arose in
the semi-darkness and unhooked the electrodes. Cipriano was asleep before she even
turned off the machine.

When he reached his console the next
morning, he sensed that there was something
different about the Eugenic Complex. He
hoped that it was merely his imagination.
Through the glass, he could see several technicians and a Bioneer working on Feraxya's
Tank.

Cipriano placed the psi-helmet on his head
and flipped the transmission switch. "I've

been expecting you," said Feraxya, instantly crowding his mind; the transmission was almost aggressive.

"What do you mean?" he said quickly.

"When you never came back yesterday, I began to worry about you. Then I felt them fumbling around my Tank. I knew something was wrong."

"I'm sorry," he said. "I was very busy yesterday. I didn't have time to—"

"Don't try to explain. I already know what they're getting ready to do."

"What? What're you talking about. How?" He looked out at the great mass of flesh, seeing it for the first time as something that could be very different from what he had always imagined.

"The night-shift Monitor told me what had happened. I forced him to do it. I wanted to know why they were tampering with me. And when he told me, I was hurt by it. Why couldn't *you* tell me, Benjamin? I didn't want that other man to tell me, but I had no choice."

"I'm sorry," was all he could manage to say.

"It hurt to know that you had run out of the Complex without telling me, Benjamin."

"Please," he said. "I understand what you're saying. And I'm sorry. I shouldn't have done it."

"Why do they call it a 'scrape'?"

"It's just slang, that's all. It doesn't mean anything. They don't do abortions that way anymore."

"Will they be coming soon?" she asked.

"I think so. Don't worry. It won't take long. You won't even feel—"

"No, Benjamin. I don't want them to do it. You've got to tell them not to do it."

Cipriano suppressed a laugh, although it was more from anxiety than from humor. "You don't want it? There isn't anything you can do about it. It's the law, Feraxya! Chicago doesn't allow random births. You know that."

"The only thing I know is that they want to destroy my brood. They want to cut me open and rip them from my flesh. It is wrong," she said slowly.

"There was a mistake in the gene-printing," said Cipriano, trying to explain things in the only way he understood. "Your fetuses aren't perfect constructs."

"But they're human beings, Benjamin. They want to murder them. I can't let them do it."

Cipriano tried to understand her feelings, her reasons for talking such nonsense to him. He began to fear that maybe she was losing control of her senses. "Why are you telling me this?" he asked finally. "You know there isn't anything I can do about it."

"You can tell them not to try. I want to give them a chance."

"They won't listen to me, Feraxya. Barstowe's already scheduled the surgery for this morning. There's nothing you can do but accept what's happening. Face the truth: you're getting an abortion." He immediately regretted the last sentence as soon as he had said it. He could almost feel the pain he was inflicting in her.

"I can't believe that's really you talking. I always thought you were *different* from the rest of them. You acted like you had more understanding, more compassion . . ."

"You make it sound like I'm against you," he said defensively.

"Perhaps you're not. But you've got to tell them that I'll stop anybody who tries to get near me. Even kill them if necessary." Feraxya's voice in his mind was sharp, cutting deeply into his skull like a bright razor.

"And you're telling me about understanding, about compassion? Feraxya, what's happening to you?" Inwardly, he reviewed her last words. What was this talk about *killing*? If her mind was going, Barstowe would have to know about it.

"I can't help it, Benjamin. It's something that I feel deep inside. Something that we've almost forgotten about. The instincts, the drive that a mother feels to protect her children."

"They're not your children," he said vindictively.

"They were given to me. They're *mine*." There was a long pause. "I don't want to argue with you. Please, go tell them what I've said."

Cipriano exhaled slowly. "All right. I'll see Barstowe, but I don't think it'll do any good."

He waited for her to reply, but when she didn't, he switched off the communications channel and pulled the helmet from his head.

He keyed in Barstowe's office, but the lines were all jammed with other calls. Wanting to get the matter finished as quickly as possible, he left the booth and walked to the elevators that would take him to Barstowe's office level.

After the Superior was given a reconstruction of the conversation, he shook his head as if in disbelief. "Nothing like this has ever happened before," the man said.

"Well, what do we do about it?" asked Cipriano.

"*Do!?*" cried Barstowe. "We don't have to do anything about it. We just ignore that crap and go on with the operation. You can tell her she'll be getting a new implantation as soon as possible."

Cipriano paused, still thinking about what she had said to him. He looked at Barstowe and spoke again: "What about that bit about 'killing' people?"

Barstowe laughed. "Just a threat . . . a very stupid one at that."

"You don't think she's more powerful than we've imagined, do you?"

"What're you getting at?" Barstowe stared at him with cold, penetrating eyes that looked like oiled ball bearings.

"*I* don't know," said Cipriano. "I just can't figure out why she'd talk like that. It's not like her."

"Well, we don't have time to worry about it. For now—" Barstowe was interrupted by the buzzer on his communicator. The man answered it, and saw a white-helmeted Bioneer on the screen. They spoke for several seconds, then the screen darked out. "That was Stander. They're about ready to get started. I want you down there. You can tell her what was said up here."

Cipriano nodded and left the office. When he returned to his console, he could see the surgical team approaching Feraxya's Tank. He put on the helmet and opened the channel to her mind. "They wouldn't listen," he said. "They're coming now. Pretty soon you'll be going under anesthesia. I'm sorry, Feraxya."

"Don't be sorry, Benjamin," was all she said. There was something chilling in the way she had touched his mind. The familiar warmness had vanished, and Cipriano felt the first twinges of terror icing in his spinal cord.

A Bioneer approached his console and prepared to administer the anesthesia. Outside the booth, Cipriano could see the surgical team as they reached the glassteel wall of the Tank. Suddenly the man next to him threw back his head and uttered a brief scream. The man tried to press his hands to his head just as blood began to stream from his nose and the corners of his mouth; the man's eyes bulged out, unseeing, and he slumped over the console dead from a massive cerebral hemorrhage. Cipriano rushed over to him but there was nothing that could be done.

Next to the Breeder Tank, the three men of the surgical team were waiting for the anesthesia to take effect. One of them had begun scaling the wall of the Tank, but he never made it. Falling backward, the man landed on his back as he struggled with his suit's helmet, convulsed for several seconds, and then lay still. The remaining two surgeons rushed to his aid, but had taken only a few steps before they, too, were struck down by some unseen, killing force.

Cipriano watched their death throes as alarms wailed through the corridors. Suddenly people were scrambling all around him. Two parameds ran into the Breeder Tank Area and were also brought down screaming and convulsing. Benjamin stepped back from the booth window, feeling a pit form at the base of his stomach. He flipped on the screen and punched for Barstowe's office. "Something's happened to the team!" he yelled before the picture materialized. "Barstowe! Can you hear me?"

The Superior's face appeared on the screen. "I know! What's going on down there? The intercom's going crazy!"

"I don't know," said Cipriano. "I don't know!"

"Who's in there with you?"

"I'm not sure. There's a lot of noise ... confusion. Some technicians, a medic."

"Put one of the techs on," said Barstowe, regaining some of his usual composure.

Cipriano called the closest man over to the communicator. Barstowe said something to the technician, who nodded and reached for the anesthesia switch. Before he threw it, blood spurted from his nose and ears, and he fell away from the console. He was dead before he hit the floor.

Backing away from the console, Benjamin looked out to the Tank of pink flesh. Now the massiveness of the thing took on a new meaning. Within its walls lurked a powerful and angry intelligence.

The screen was signaling, but there was no one close enough to answer it. Wiping the perspiration from his face, Cipriano edged close to the screen and saw Barstowe's searching eyes. "Get out of there!" the Superior screamed. "I'm calling back all the emergency units. Get up here right now." The screen blacked out.

Quickly, Cipriano shouldered his way through the crowd of Complex guards and Bioneers and headed for the nearest elevator. When he reached Barstowe's office, he found the man in animated conversation in front of his communicator. Seeing Cipriano, the Superior flicked off the screen and spoke to him: "Chicago's Central Computers postulates some kind of limited-range telekinetic power—an unexpected variable of the psi-training."

"I thought it would be something like that," said Benjamin. "What do you want with me?"

"You seem to have gotten along with her reasonably well in the past," said Barstowe, pausing for dramatic effect. "And she seemed to leave you alone down there just now."

"And . . . ?"

"Get in touch with her again. Try to reason with her. Calm her down. Tell her anything. Tell her that we've capitulated, that we won't abort her brood. Anything, I don't care what."

"I don't understand," said Cipriano.

"You don't have to understand it. Just do what you're told." Barstowe stood up from his desk and faced him squarely. "We want you to divert her attention, keep her occupied until we can rig up a bypass away from your console to the Breeder Tank."

"A bypass? What're you talking about?" Cipriano asked, although he already had an idea of what Barstowe intended.

"We're going to try and shut her down from outside the Complex. Shunt from the Central Computer."

"You mean you're going to *kill* her?"

"You're goddamn right we are!" Barstowe screamed. "Listen, Chicago has postulated what would happen if that thing downstairs can somehow communicate with the other Host-Mothers. If the combined psi powers of the entire Breeder Tank Area could be coordinated, their power would be awesome. We can't let some kind of matrix like that materialize. Now get out of here."

Cipriano rode down to his level and returned once more to the console. The entire area was deserted and his footsteps echoed down the corridor adjoining his booth. Barstowe's words were also echoing through his mind. Thoughts of Feraxya, of the other Host-Mothers, of the men who'd been killed, of the entire nightmarish scene all swarmed through his mind like a cloud of devouring insects. He felt helplessly trapped in the middle of a conflict that he wanted no part of.

He sat down and put on the helmet. As he threw on the proper switch, he could feel her mind lurking nearby, waiting for him to speak. "You've changed, Feraxya," he said finally.

"Why did you come back?" she said.

"I don't know," he lied. "There was nothing else to do."

"What are they going to do with me, Benjamin?"

"I . . . don't know." Again, he lied. And this time it was painful. Adrenaline pumped through him; his hands were trembling. He was glad that she could not see him.

"Do you understand why I had to do it?" she asked. "You know I didn't want it this way."

"No, I don't understand. You've become a murderer, Feraxya."

"I didn't want to do it. I just wanted to protect my brood. They have as much right to live as you or me. I won't let them be killed." Her voice in his mind seemed strained, tense. Perhaps her mind *was* going. He shuddered as he thought of what an insane horror she could become.

"What are you going to do now?" he asked. "They've evacuated the entire Complex. But they'll be back. You can't hold out like this forever, you know."

"I don't know, Benjamin. I'm scared. You know I'm scared. If they would promise to leave me alone, to leave my brood alone, I won't hurt them. My duty to the Society is to produce new Citizens. That's what I want to do. That's all. You believe me, don't you?"

"Yes, I believe you," said Cipriano just as he was distracted by several flashing lights on his console. He hadn't touched any of the switches; the technicians must be activating the controls through the recently rigged by-pass circuits. He knew what was going to happen.

"Benjamin, are you still there . . . ? What's wrong?"

"I'm sorry," he said quickly, while his mind raced ahead, envisioning what would come next. He was of two minds, one of which wanted to cry out, to warn her of what was planned, the other that was content to sit back and witness her execution. He heard himself talking: ". . . and you've got to trust us, Feraxya. You can't keep killing everybody. There would be no one to maintain your systems. Everyone would lose in the end." Watching the console, Cipriano recognized the symbols that now blazed in bright scarlet on the message grid. They were planning to terminate.

"All right, Benjamin . . ." Feraxya's words were echoing through his brain. "I'll—"

Her words were cut short. Cipriano jumped up from the chair, his eyes on the great Breeder Tank. The console chattered and flickered as it processed the remote commands being fed into it. "Feraxya!" he screamed as he realized what was happening, what she must now know. A life-support systems graph appeared on the grid; the plot lines all began dropping toward the y-coordinate. His mind was flooded with her last thoughts—surprise, panic, loathing, and pain. For a moment he thought he felt her icy, telekinetic grip reaching out to him, enclosing cold fingers about his brain. The seconds

ticked by with glacier-like slowness. His
mind lay in a dark pit of fear as he awaited
her retribution.

The life-fluids and the oxygen were cut
off, and the great amorphous body convulsed
within the Breeder Tank. She reached out
and touched his mind for the last time, but
in fear rather than anger or hate. She forced
him to experience her death. Cipriano closed
his eyes against the vicarious pain, unable to
wrench the helmet from his head.

Then suddenly it was over. A gathering
darkness filled him. The console had begun
force-feeding acid through her circulatory
system, bubbling away the flesh, ensuring
that she was gone.

The communicator screen grew into
brightness and Barstowe's face appeared
there. The Superior was smiling, but Benjamin ripped off the helmet and left the console
before the man spoke. The corridor outside
his booth was again filled with people, their
voices loud with celebration and relief. He
ignored their backslapping and shouldered
past them to the descent elevators.

He kept wondering why she had touched
him like that, at the end. Had she known?
Did she think it was he who was killing her?

He left the Complex under the weight of
his thoughts. Outside, Chicago sparkled under night sky. Its sidewalks and transit systems were filling up with work-wearied
crowds who sought entertainment in the
City. Cipriano stepped onto a slidewalk that
carried him through the midsection of the

urban complex. He was in no hurry to go home now.

Ahead of him, the walk snaked through a kaleidoscope forest of color and light, through the pleasure-center of the City—Xanadu. The crowds were heavy here, each seeking the mindless relief that was always to be found in this Sector. Cipriano studied them as he threaded his way through the mobs. They were all born of Host-Mothers like Feraxya, all laughing and playing their games of escape, oblivious to their grotesque origins. He passed a series of Fantasy Parlors where the lines were already long. The patrons were mostly lower-level Citizens—nontechs, laborers, and drones—that filled this Sector. They were all eager to use the City's computers to immerse themselves in imaginary worlds. Sexual fantasies were a major part of the catalog. Cipriano knew this as he passed the other opiate-dispensing centers: the mind-shops, elec-droug centers, and other "pleasure domes." The brightness of the lights assaulted him with their vulgar screams, the polished steel and reflecting glass shimmered with a special kind of tawdriness. For the first time, perhaps, Cipriano realized a terrible truth: the City was unable to provide for all of man's needs. There was something missing, something primal and liberating, something that was now only a desiccated memory out of man's dark history.

Perhaps Feraxya, too, was aware of the deficiency, he thought. Perhaps that would help to explain what he had first thought to be her irrational action. He closed his eyes against the argon-brightness, frustrated because his questions would forever be unanswered.

The slidewalk moved on, taking him away from the entertainment Sector. He entered a corridor of glassteel spires—Chicago's con-apt Sectors. Cipriano untangled the matrix of walks and ramps and lifts which led to his building, and reluctantly ascended to his con-apt level. Before he could palm the homeostatic lock, Jennifer was at the door, her face a portrait of concern. All the media had been blurting out the news of the near-catastrophe at the Eugenic Complex; she already knew what he had been forced to do.

During dinner, she pressed him for details, which he produced grudgingly in short clipped sentences. Even Jennifer could perceive his lack of enthusiasm. "Perhaps I can help," she said.

At first he did not understand, for his mind was not really listening to her. Only after she had stood up from the table and taken a few steps toward the bedroom did he fully comprehend: she wished to console him in the only manner that she knew.

He felt cold. The memory of Feraxya's last moments of life passed through him like winter's breath. He could feel her reaching through the darkness, trying until the very end to make him *know* her, choosing him to be cursed with her memory.

Jennifer called his name.

Feraxya's image shattered like broken glass, and he felt himself rising from his chair, entering the bedroom. A solitary candle burned there, where Jennifer sat making cursory adjustments on the machine. Turning, she reached out and began to undress him. Mechanically, he did the same for her.

As her clothes fell away, revealing her warm, silky flesh, he suddenly saw her differently. Instead of reaching for the wired bands and electrodes, Cipriano extended his hand and touched one of her breasts. For a moment, she was transfixed, frozen by his action. His hand slowly moved, cupping the fullness in his hand, brushing her nipple with his fingers.

He felt it swell and become rigid as she spoke: "No ... no! Oh, please, Benjamin ... don't. Please . . ."

"But why?" he asked as he removed his hand. But inwardly he was still marveling at the softness of her.

"Not like that," she was saying. "The machine. We *can't*. Not without the machine."

Something dark and ugly roiled inside his mind. He wanted to challenge her, to break through her defenses with his reckless anomie. But when he looked into her haunted eyes and saw the fear and disbelief that lay there, he knew that he could not.

She could not be touched. In either sense.

Lying down, he let her attach the electrodes, felt her recline beside him. The humming of the machine rose in intensity, crowding out his thoughts. Sensations seeped into him, sending slivers of pleasures into the maelstrom of his mind's center. Vaguely, he was aware of Jennifer writhing beside him, arching her body upward as the stimulations increased. His own desires, finally awakened, snaked through him, radiating out from his groin, threatening to strangle him with their grasp. He resisted the electronic impulses, and focused his mind's eye upon the Breeder Tank where Feraxya floated in the jellied sea, where she had been able to touch him, perhaps even love him, as no one had ever done before.

Jennifer increased the attenuator, forcing the machine to drive them to unusual, even for her, frenzy. The energy-burst overwhelmed him as he finally succumbed to the wave of pleasure collapsing over him.

Feraxya faded from his thoughts as he tripped through a series of orgasms.

Not all men are lured into the metallic web. There are still those who have not been absorbed by the machines, and they look to the stars. Perhaps because the City knows this to be a final reaching, a futile dying act, it acquiesces.

FOUR

Shafts of sunlight danced on the choppy surface of the lake. Beyond its broken brightness lay the City—a clutch of spires and spheres, tesseracts and towers. It was like a Mondrian painting of three-dimensional geometrics, reaffirming itself through color and light. Miria studied its random compositions from the vantage point of the flivver which skimmed tantalizingly above the whitecaps, rushing toward the IASA installation twenty kilometers offshore.

The installation was an impressive sight in itself, and although dwarfed in size by Chicago, it still sprawled across the surface of the lake like a floating city. An immense platform of concrete and exotic alloys, punctuated by gracefully curving ramps, soaring control towers, and an occasional thicket of atmospheric ships poised on thin legs like insects. Somewhere on the platform, thought Miria, was a shuttle that would be taking Alen up to the starship.

Today was the day she could finally see him again. All the tests and training and conditioning programs had been run and the final selections for the crew had been made.

Alen had called her earlier in the day, at the City's monstrous Information Retrieval Center, where she had been cataloging and encoding a Rimbaud anthology for the crystal databanks. He still did not know when he would be leaving.

The flivver gravved up to the quay and passengers began to rise from their seats. Miria slipped into the flow, raising her ID bracelet as they passed through the Security portal leading into the terminal. From there, she sought out a routing display and selected the necessary sequence of walks that would carry her to the astronaut's residence sector. As she rode the walks, she self-consciously adjusted her gown—an organically cultured film that flowed liquidly over her body, reflecting a diffused lime-tinted light. She wore her blond hair long and loose because she had seen pictures of Dante Rossetti's women and they had looked like that. She paid little attention to the daily-changing fashions of the City, and at times she honestly believed she would have been a happier woman in the nineteenth century.

Reaching the residence sector, she was again cleared by Security and admitted into the maze of corridors and intersecting elevator shafts. His suite was twelve levels beneath surface and the elevator, although descending rapidly, seemed slow when paced with her anxieties. She found his door quickly and palmed the lock, he having already coded it for her heat-signature. Alen was seated in a contour chair—a mock antique of the early twentieth. His face was squarish, lips thin, eyes wide apart and green-flecked gold. He was wearing a functional robe and the illumination from the uncoded wall-screens cast an even, dull glow across his depilated skull. If Miria looked closely she could see the marks left by the implants and the sensors.

Alen stood up and greeted her with a smile.

"I came as fast as I could," she said. "The crowds were thick during the change of shifts."

"It's all right. I was resting. Sit down."

She joined him on a couch covered with ersatz leather. "When?"

He shook his head. "I'm not sure. There will still be time, though. The selection of the passenger list, the specialists, and the construction crews will take a long time. Don't forget, all the people who are chosen will have to be replaced somewhere in the system."

Miria nodded. "Have they selected the star?"

"Not exactly. The ship is going to the Central Cluster. Lots of star systems to choose from there."

Miria thought of the great ship rushing through the emptiness with the whole universe as a backdrop, carrying a ragged piece of humanity to an unknown fate. It was both a beautiful and a terrible vision. "When I think about it, it's hard to believe it's really going to happen. There's such a finality about it, Alen."

The astronaut shook his head, frowning.

"What else can we do? Everywhere you look, there's nothing but dead ends for us here. We've been to all the planets and back for more than a century now. There's nothing out there, except those things on Jupiter, and after seventy years, we *still* can't be sure whether or not they're even sentient."

"But just for the sake of exploring ... of expanding. I mean, is that all the reason there is?"

"Miria, we've been through this before. I've been created to be an astronaut. I never really had a choice. No one ever does, *you* know that. I was made to spend my days out there. If they want me to go to the stars, I go."

She looked at him for a long time before saying anything. His ruddy complexion was creased and burned and he looked far older than he actually was. And his eyes looked older still. She could sense something lurking behind his eyes that intimated thoughts other than what he had said. "That's not all, Alen. I can tell. I know you."

"You know a lot of people have had enough down here," he said softly, evenly, as though he was angry with her.

Miria could only nod her head. She herself was a sympathizer of several underground organizations that advocated less technology and less control over the individual lives of the Citizens. She knew that since all the powers of the western hemisphere had formed the loosely connected alliance, the NorAm Confederation, the security of mankind had become less stable instead of more secure. The rise of antiquarian fashions and nostalgic flirtations was more than just a society's cyclic turns. It was no coincidence that the number of "flyers"—those who simply walked away from their assignments, their homes, their friends, and disappeared, presumably to join the small villages and agricultural regions that still clung to the earth despite the rise of the Mega cities—had significantly increased year by year for more than a generation.

"There's a lot of free spirits here," said Alen, as if he could touch her thoughts. "It's natural, I guess, among the bunch that's been ... away from the Earth. It's different out there. There's a freedom you feel that just doesn't exist down here."

"It's not going to get any better," she said. "The Confederation is a joke. I keep having the feeling that if another war comes, it's going to be everyone for himself."

"Why not? Look at the cities—they're getting to be like little nations themselves."

"The Greeks," she said, pausing.

"What?"

"The Greeks, the same thing happened to them. They were a fascinating race, you know. Talking about the power of the atom thousands of years ago, writing philosophies that are still viable. And yet they splintered themselves up into little city-states, even had wars among themselves."

"Well, we haven't come to that yet," said Alen, forcing a smile to his lips. It was a pathetic gesture.

"No, but it could happen. And we're not going to be able to stop it if it does."

"We can stop it, Miria. Even if only by walking away from it. What would we be losing? What will *I* be losing? The possibility of having even more freedoms taken away? Did you know they're playing with the idea of *predicting* deviants? You know, screening us all at particular 'developmental stages' to see if we're falling into any patterns that will lead to criminal behavior?"

"What? Alen, that's ridiculous."

"I'm sure that's exactly what people said when they talked about genetically designing whole classes of people, too." He stood up and turned away from her, his hands were clenched into fists and the back of his naked neck was flushed.

"Where did you hear about it?" She didn't want to continue the thread of the conversation if it was going to upset him, but her curiosity compelled her to do so.

"There's a lot of cybernetic people at the installation, Miria. Consultants, specialists, designers, even techs. They all get around. You know, crosstalk between the computer people over in Central. They're working on all sorts of things you wouldn't believe. Sooner or later, true Artificial Intelligence will be a reality. Machines that are no longer merely machines. Machines that can *really* think, not just carry out a chain of commands."

Alen pulled the robe more tightly around him, began pacing across the thick carpet. "One of the techs was talking to me just a few days ago, while I was finishing up my course work, and he tells me that he's been assigned to a new project already, as soon as our ship leaves. Seems like he's going to be trying to dream up better ways of keeping the population satisfied with their lives."

"That sounds like a psychologist's work, not a cybernetic man."

"Perhaps. Frankly, these guys scare the shit out of me. It sounds like more kinds of *control*, Miria. And control means infringing upon our freedom."

"Freedom's an illusion," she said. "Nobody's really free."

"The 'flyers' are free. *I* will be free." The words were spoken with a sneer, as if they could be insulting and condescending.

She only looked at him, unsure of how to interpret what he meant.

"Hey, I'm sorry. I didn't mean it like that," he said, reading her confused, half-hurt expression. "I didn't mean it to sound like I wasn't including you."

"Alen, I want to be with you." She reached out and took his hand.

"I know you do." He kissed her forehead as she leaned against him.

"What are the chances?"

"It depends upon how many people apply for the berths. I don't know. There's a lot of factors. Age, skills, value to the City, scores on the performance and aptitude tests, lots of things. I think they'll be pretty selective."

"I haven't even applied yet," she said. "I didn't want to commit myself until I knew for sure that you were going to be in the crew."

"I'll talk to Hast in the morning. He's one of the IASA Class Ones on the project. His jurisdiction is only for the crew, but he might be able to tell if there's anybody I can talk to about the passenger and colonist list."

"Do you really think that would make any difference, Alen? I mean, there's so little human judgment involved. Isn't that the supposed 'beauty' of the whole project—the pure objectivity of it all?"

"You're worrying about it too much. Stop thinking about it until you have to. Key in an application tomorrow and wait until they've started testing you." He lifted her chin gently, then kissed her.

"You're right, I'm sorry. I must sound like an old woman."

"That's pushing things a bit." He smiled.

"Do you have to stay here again tonight?"

"Yeah, but only to check out in the morning. The program's over."

"So do I have to wait until tomorrow night, or do you think they wouldn't mind me staying awhile?" she said with a mischievous grin.

Alen smiled. "Oh, I don't think they'd mind at all."

Miria stood up, glided across the room toward his sleeping quarters, her hand at the clasp of her gown.

In the morning Alen accompanied her back to the City, he to their shared con-apt, she to her assignment at the Library Com-

plex—the Information Retrieval Center. The
structure was a black monolith, featureless
and polished, dark as the midnight; and although it was surrounded by even taller
buildings, it loomed large and impressive.
Deep within its corridors, Miria returned to
Rimbaud and his magical, twisted lines of
sound and sense. She loved the poetry of the
earlier ages, especially the mystical and the
romantic schools. It was through the influence of Shelley, Coleridge, Byron, and their
associates that Miria had come to terms with
her own perceptions of the world. She
learned to see things as others had when the
world was a calmer place, when there was
more beauty in the world.

But it was D. H. Lawrence who taught her
of love, the forgotten pleasures of physical
love. Through his poems and his haunting,
darkly sensuous stories, she imagined a world
of people who were *alive*, who knew they
were alive, and who knew how to celebrate
that aliveness.

She had met Alen when both of them
were living in a Pre-Assignment Sector, where
the Learning/Conditioning Complexes were
found, where the elite classes attended the
Multiversity Complex, where young minds
were shaped and bodies trained. And they
spent several years of learning to know each
other, taking the time, when few still did, to
give of themselves in order to receive from
the other. Although they did not know it at
the time, they were somehow different from
the others.

It was not until she was older that Miria

realized how different she was. Perhaps it was the sheer size of the City, perhaps it was the autonomous character of the technology which subconsciously molded their world, but whatever the reason, the Citizens were losing touch with each other. Chicago was a bright and shining place filled with moving, shadowy figures. It was an isle of deadened souls who touched nothing and would not be touched. Miria had never grown accustomed to an age where people thought only of themselves.

Whenever she was assigned a poet to datalog, she always took the time to read his work. She always took the time to think of Alen. She *would* be with him when he left for the stars. Any other future was unthinkable.

And so she applied to the various agencies that must approve her for the colony ship. She spent hours in front of a terminal keying in a thousand requests, a thousand data-codes, a thousand references and cross-indexes, all of which pooled together somewhere within the crystalbanks of the Central Computer Complex and described the being called Miria. After a week of this, she was called in for a battery of real-time examinations and tests.

Finally she was to be interviewed by an IASA official.

Miria sat quietly in an office of contemporary decor; walls were illuminated with holographic vistas of the cityscape. Although the view was impressive, to Miria it was indicative of a dull, uninspired mind. She, for instance, never dialed up contemporary scenes in her own con-apt. She was thinking of the magnificent view of Castle Tintagel she currently enjoyed at home when a panel slid open and the official entered the room.

He was tall and thin, very pale, looking very air-conditioned and unreal. He wore an Agency uniform that was functional in its simplicity. His eyes were gray and seemed to be unfocused even as he looked at her and spoke.

"Miria Soltan?" he said, as he seated himself behind the desk and punched in a terminal, studying its display.

She was startled for a moment—it was very rare that anyone used her referent name—and paused before answering affirmatively.

"My name is Singh. I'm sorry to have to call you in like this, but there were some questions the Agency would like to have answered that did not seem to correlate on any of our tests."

"You mean you don't interview all the applicants?"

Singh grinned feebly. "No, no. Of course not. There's not enough time. No reason, either. The machines do a nice job screening out the unacceptables."

"Oh, I see."

"Now, your Assignment is in the IRC, you are a datalogger."

"That's right."

"And yet you wish to be a member of the colony ship? In what capacity?"

Miria sensed the condescension in his voice, but chose not to react against it. "I thought I made that clear on the application program? If as nothing else, as a laborer. Or a breeder."

Singh nodded. "Yes, that's what you have keyed in here. But tell me, Soltan, what do you mean by a 'laborer'? Or a 'breeder'?"

"If the ship finds a new world, there will be years of primary work to be done. A settlement would have to be built, the territory mapped, the agriculture established, you know—a million things. Surely there must be some simple work I could do. And then there are future generations, I could be a mother."

"That's very quaint. But not very realistic. You are not going to be riding in a Conestoga wagon, however. There will be machines to do the 'labor,' as you must realize. And if the only thing you want is to contribute to the gene pool, we can arrange to have your germ plasma included among the ship's eugenic stores."

"What are you trying to say?"

"I'm saying that although your reasons for wishing to be on the ship are wholly unacceptable, we found the specific *oddness* of your reasons required a personal interview."

"You mean I cannot go?" Miria felt a flash of heat throughout her body. There was thickness in her throat, a numbness in her skull.

"Soltan, your skills as a dataloger are hardly needed on a colony ship. *No one* on board is being selected merely for his physical labor characteristics. *No one* will be bearing children on the colony world."

She felt tears in the corners of her eyes, but

she sat rigidly in the chair, fighting them back. "Then why did you call me in here? Why didn't you just flash the rejection across my terminal? Why did you have to ... humiliate me like this?"

"Our records indicate that you have been cohabiting with an astronaut—a one Alen Kinert. Our records also show that you have remained with Kinert for a period of *five years*. Is this correct?"

Suddenly the tears lay drying on her cheeks and she felt indignant rage. "Yes, it is correct! There's nothing illegal in that, is there?"

Singh smiled weakly. "Oh, no, of course not. Although I would say it's a bit peculiar, wouldn't you?"

"What?" Miria looked at him.

"Astronaut Kinert is a member of the starship crew. The reason you wish to be among the colonists is your desire to be with Kinert," said Singh. It was not a question.

"Is there something wrong with that?" Miria had lost his train of thought, his thread of logic.

"Wrong? No. Odd? Very, I'd say. *Why*, Soltan? Why would you be willing to throw away a high-level Assignment to face hell-knows-what out there. Just to be with another person? It doesn't add up."

"I'm sorry but it's true," she said simply, bowing her head. When Singh did not immediately reply, she felt the urge to explain herself, to attempt to describe the relationship she and Alen enjoyed. But she knew there was no use in that. What for? Would it make things any different? She knew that it would not. No, the decision had long ago been made that she would not ride the starship. Alen would be taken away from her and she would never see him again. It was that simple, that cruelly simple.

"I see," said Singh finally. "Then why did you not state this . . . involvement with Kinert as your motivation for joining the mission?"

Miria looked up at the pale man. "Because I knew it would not be a sufficient reason. I knew it would draw the exact kind of surprise and disbelief that you are showing me."

Singh smiled. "Yes, well, at least you seem to have things in proper perspective. I'm sorry that your application has been rejected, I really am. But you must realize, this selection process is a difficult one. The starship was not one of the contingencies in the Eugenics program of the last two generations. There were *no* Citizens specifically bred for colonization. That meant that everyone would have to be pulled from existing Assignments and that the qualifications for the crew and passenger list would have to be very carefully screened. I'm sure you understand this, and the Agency would like to thank you for your interest and willingness to sacrifice for the sake of the mission."

Singh stood up and extended his hand. Shaking it automatically, Miria said nothing and turned away quickly. Her only thought was that she wanted to get away from the place as quickly as possible.

Alen met her at a Rapids terminal and they rode above the Traffic lanes toward the west. The vehicle grew less crowded at every stop as they approached the terminus of the line. They frequently rode the Rapids to the extreme limits of the City, beyond which was the land of the Confederation Preserves set aside for the vast agricultural complexes.

Stepping down from the station, they rented an electricar and passed beyond a checkpoint onto one of the monitored highways. Alen transpared the windows and they both stared out into the immense emptiness of the agricultural plains. The sky was a swirl of dusk-colors: purple, gray, burnt orange. In the distance the undulating grain was occasionally punctuated by the great shadowy shape of a foodprocessor wading through the crops like an all-devouring beast.

Miria looked at Alen, started to speak, and then checked herself. They had spoken very little on the Rapids. Neither of them seemed to know what to say. Something alien had come between them, something which sought to defeat their intimacy.

Alen had keyed in coordinates that were familiar to both of them. Three years before, they had discovered some rolling countryside which looked down upon a verdant river valley beyond the agricultural preserve. Several anachronistic villages lay sleepily there and farming was done without foodprocessors. As the car sped silently toward that spot, Alen leaned back and looked at her. "We should count our blessings, actually," he said, trying to smile.

"What do you mean?"

"Someday, I'll bet that people won't even be able to do this, to leave the City like this."

"Why not?"

"Lots of reasons. It might get too dangerous. Or they might finally get around to building those force-fields, the energy domes."

"God, I hope not."

"It might be the only way to survive an all-out war. They might be forced to do it."

"Alen, that doesn't matter anymore," she said as she turned and looked angrily at him. Her eyes were glistening and she could feel a cold moisture in the palms of her hands.

"No, I suppose it doesn't," was all he could say, sensing her desperate bitterness.

"How long will it take? How long before you get there?"

"You mean ship-time? Or down here?"

"Either. Both, I guess."

"It all depends upon whether or not the ship will be able to maintain a one-gravity acceleration. It could take between fifty and one hundred years—ship-time."

"Fifty to a hundred years? But Alen, you'd be—"

"Dead? No. The crew will be in coldsleep for most of the voyage, just like the colonists. We'll all be revived for short maintenance shifts on a rotating basis. I probably won't be awake for more than six or seven years." He reached out and took her hand, squeezing it tightly.

"And . . . how much time will pass here?"

"A long time, Miria."

"*How* long?"

"Close to a hundred thousand years," he said, looking into bottomless blue eyes.

Miria looked away from him, through the car's windows at the Preserve, where great splashes of an impressionistic color waved in the wind. A hundred thousand years, she thought. What would this all be like then? What would it be like? It was doubtful that man would last that long. She thought briefly about that far future when Alen would have aged only a few years, when even the dust of her bones would no longer remain. A shudder ran through her, a feeling of vast emptiness, as she contemplated her non-existence. And she thought of how unfair the universe could be, how insensitive and seemingly without purpose life appeared.

She did not speak for what seemed like a long time. Alen, sensing her state of mind, respected her silence and did not intrude, until at last the car reached its coordinates, rolling to a gradual stop.

Opening the doors, he led her out to a grassy knoll which overlooked the Preserve. Beyond it, through the shifting light of dusk, she could see the City, looking like a tiny formation of amethyst crystals growing randomly across a mossy cavern floor.

"From here, it does not seem so imposing," said Alen softly, his voice dying quickly in the evening air.

"Everyone should see it like this. Perhaps the City would be different then."

"I've felt the same thing in space. Out there, you see the Earth differently. The stars can do strange things, too."

"I remember reading about a man named Link," said Miria, as she lay on her back, watching the stars blink into view as the last shards of day shattered and lay scattered across the far horizon.

"A famous story," said Alen. "He was one of the first starship pilots. They were experimenting with cyborgs back then. When they brought him in, he was crazy as a rat."

"What happened to him?"

"He eventually recovered, I think. That was back when the Government still exhibited some care over its heroes. They learned a lot from Link. No more cyborgs, they said. And they meant it for a while."

"What do you mean?"

"There's talk of cyborg technology making a comeback. Maybe not for starflight, but other things."

"It sounds horrible."

"I'm sure it is. They say that you become more than a man, but some say that you become much less."

She reached out and touched his face, pale and graven in the stark half shadows of the starlight. "I love you, Alen. I love you very much."

He nodded but did not reply. He must have known what she was thinking. Thinking that soon she would never see him again, that she would be left in a place that seemed to live without love, and did not seem to suffer from its absence.

And then he was kissing her, touching her, bringing her body to life and warmth in the chill of the evening. It was fitting that they should spend one of their last times together in this place; she remembered the sweetness of the first time they had come there. She had been so young, and yet so full of the dreams like the poets, of the reveries of the past, and she had seduced him like Salome, like Cleopatra, like Helen, like the unnamed lover of Housman's Shropshire lad.

Afterward, she lay in his arms, smelling the sweetness of his sweat, feeling the warmth of his legs entwined in hers, trying not to think of a future beyond that moment. She would have been satisfied never to speak another word to him. There was nothing to say that would better express the love which she gave him that night. The silence comforted her, warmed her, and she was almost upset when Alen broke it.

"There's a way," he said softly into her ear. "There's a way, Miria."

"What? What are you talking about?" She looked up at him and saw that he was smiling.

He sat up, draping his shirt over her shoulders, pulling her close to him. "The answer's so plain, so obvious, I should have realized it before."

"What do you mean? Tell me, Alen."

And he did.

The preparations and the bureaucratic entanglements seemed endless, but Alen, by virtue of his Class One status and his connections at the installation, was able to push through the impediments, circumvent the barricades. And so he stood by Miria's bed deep within the leveled City, so deep that there were only a handful of levels beneath them, down where the great fusion reactors generated the limitless quantities of plasma energy which powered the City.

"The shuttle doesn't leave for three days yet," said Miria. "Why must I be here now? There's still time, Alen."

He smiled and shook his head. "Don't talk about time, now. We have enough of that. Besides, I have a million hours of briefings before lift-off. My three days will be like a thousand. I wouldn't have been able to see you anyhow."

"Will you stay with me until ... until the end?" She reached out from beneath the liquid-like sheet and sought his hand.

"Of course. Of course I will. They'll be coming soon. Don't worry."

"Does it hurt? Will I feel it? Will I know anything?"

He shook his head. "I've been through it during the training. Nothing to it."

"I can still be scared, can't I?"

"You can be anything you want to be," he said, smiling.

The sound of a door irising open behind him heralded the approach of two technicians. They nodded stiffly to Alen and began rolling Miria's bed toward the other end of the room, where another door hissed open at their approach. She listened for his footsteps and, knowing that he followed, she felt more secure.

She was taken into a larger room whose walls reflected the illumination of several

consoles and databoards. Someone peeled the
sheet from her naked body. She felt instantly
cold and exposed and very vulnerable. A
machine was lowered close to her. There was
a humming sound and the device slowly
passed over her length, leaving her flesh dancing lightly on the edge of numbness. Then
she was lifted from the bed and passed into a
container that was transparent and rectangular except for the underside, which was soft
and made of material that conformed to the
shape of her body. She felt drowsy and listless
and her limbs heavy. Somewhere in the mists
that seemed to be swirling up into her mind,
she grasped for the image and the thought of
Alen. She wanted to touch him once more, to
tell him one more time ...

Turning her head was the greatest effort,
but she accomplished this and saw him standing beyond the ranks of the technicians. He
seemed to be moving, wavering, shimmering.
But she told herself that this could not be so;
it must be the effect of the process. She tried
to speak, but that power was lost to her and
she felt an ache beneath the numbness that
was sinking into her.

I will wait now, she thought to him. I
will wait for you.

And then the side of the transparent tank
was closed, and the atmosphere changed sub-
tly and slowly. Her eyes slid shut and the rise
and fall of her breasts became regular and
steady and ever slower. Alen remained by her
until the technicians moved the tank into the
central cryogenic chamber.

From an observation terrace, Alen watched

as, minutes later, they entered the enormous chamber. It was like an endless hall of tiny rectangular mirrors lying on the long sides, but if one looked beyond the shining glass, one could see the shadowy, insubstantial shapes beyond. How long had some of them lain in suspension? There was no way of knowing when cures to their esoteric illnesses would be perfected. No way of knowing for any of them, except Miria, thought Alen. Her deliverance would come from the stars.

The three days of briefing passed quickly. The City hardly noticed when the shuttle lifted off from the lake. While Alen rode atop the flickering pencil of light and heat, a woman lay beneath the City in the darkness of coldsleep, a smile upon her face.

The last starships are only a flickering memory. Knowing this, the City concedes its meager losses and consolidates its gains. The population must be served; the City must continue. With the aid of brilliant servant/masters, the City searches for new ways to accomplish its goals.

FIVE

"Love is madness. Did you know that?"
asked the voice. Feminine. Soft. Almost a
whisper.

He nodded and tried to swallow, but found
it difficult. The room was dark except for a
polyhedron which shimmered in the center.
He recognized it as an unfocused holograph-
ic nexus, and waited for it to resolve itself
into something.

The something was her. She was naked.
And she was surrounded by, enveloped by, at
one with the flames.

"Come to me," she said. "I will demon-
strate."

The spire seemed to be alive, burning
briefly as bright as the Shields themselves.
Lucas stood in the assault bay of the
hovercraft, watching the thousand-meter
column of glassteel as it spurted gouts of fire
and smoke into the antiseptic air. There was
a knot tightening in the pit of his stomach,
squeezing at his viscera like a closed fist.
Soon he would confront the fiery beast; the
knot would loosen, and descend. As the ship
edged closer to the great building, he heard

the pilot's voice exchanging information with Chicago's computers, which orchestrated the swarm of hovercraft. Behind him, Lucas felt the press of the other firemen's bodies, smelled their perspiration and their fear.

Angling closer to the curtainwall, the hovercraft extended a grabber-ramp which attached itself to the side of the burning tower. There was a momentary lurch and Lucas almost fell. Regaining his balance, he and the others ran quickly across the ramp and cut through the glassteel face with laser torches. They stepped into a corridor obscured by roiling clouds of black smoke.

Lucas rechecked his visor seals and respirator valves as he felt the first waves of superheated air through his protective suit. Around him, men were scrambling furiously to uncoil hoses, release valves, rig equipment. He ached to see the beast, to feel its fierce breath and enter its dark veils. He could feel his heartbeat increase, his blood throbbing at his temples.

Shouting a series of commands, Lucas led a troop of firemen down a maze of twisting corridors until they reached the leading edge of the flames. For a moment, Lucas stood transfixed as he stared into the face of the firewall, which danced and raged like an elemental mistress. Hoses were brought up and Lucas fought to control the nozzle of one as it began to explode in a rush of water. Lucas directed the spray into the center of the flames, but accidentally brushed the nozzle against his right leg. Immediately he was more intensely aware of the synthaflesh panty-hose which he wore beneath his turn-out gear. It gave him pleasure as he searched in the flames for a sign of confirmation. Lucas smiled as his erection grew full and throbbing.

The fire reluctantly pulled back from the cascading attack, giving up scorched territory and attempting to escape into the ceiling-work which led to the next level. Lucas and his men extended grapplers from their fighting rigs and tore into the suspended ceiling, trying to rob the fire of its fuel. His breath raced in and out and his arms grew weary. His mind fought against an odd darkness of doubt. Somewhere in the darkness, he knew, there was a two-headed phoenix taking alternating bites of his id: one of pleasure, one of pain.

One of the firemen's grapplers became snarled in the wire lattice of the ceiling-work, and an entire section of the charred, flaming ceiling ripped loose and sliced down toward them. Lucas reacted quickly enough, jumping back and almost tripping over the tangle of hoses at his feet. But one of his men was not so fortunate and was pinned beneath the fiery section as it crashed to the floor of the corridor. The fireman's screams were muffled by the sealed visor of his helmet, his writhing, kicking movements soon muffled by the searing blanket of wreckage. Lucas extended a grappler and together with several other men pulled the ceiling-work from the fallen man. It yielded and uncovered a still form, the alloy-fabric of his turn-out rig blistered and cracked, the body within effectively parboiled.

Someone radioed for a medic and Lucas stood helplessly watching the fireman be dragged away to an awaiting hovercraft. As he turned back to the flames, a thought chilled through him, insulating him momentarily from the battle-heat. Desire ebbed away as he imagined what would happen if he himself should be injured. He shuddered as he pictured himself lying helpless in a medicsector as they peeled his gear from his body and discovered the panty-hose. They would not understand.

There was a blur of activity about him. Blinking, Lucas returned his attention to fire. He stared into the creature's face and was once more consumed by it, cherishing the excitement that was again swelling within.

There were filaments attached to his skull. He could feel them snaking Medusa-like away from his head, gathering and twisting themselves into a thick cable which burrowed into a large console. His eyelids did not move—could not move. Images coalesced and danced before him and he felt heat, moisture, and sliding scales of passion. He did these things for several lifetimes until there was finally an end to it all. The voice of the Occupational Therapist echoed through his skull: "Work is love. Did you know that?"

Lucas acquired the habit of taking showers while wearing his helmet and turn-out coat. It was difficult to imagine how he had existed before discovering such pleasures. The warm water splashed against his faceplate, running down his neck and over his chest. He swirled soap over his body until he was so slippery that he could not resist masturbating into the cleansing cascade.

Afterward he would lie in the solitude of the bedroom in a half sleep, trying to ignore the creeping doubts, the subdural flashes of guilt. His life was changing. His *Weltanschauung* was being surgically altered, and he was a casual witness to the event. Perhaps, he thought at such times, he needed a more potent anesthetic.

But of course the room was cold, without real warmth, and therefore without love.

He lay quietly in the Debriefing Chamber—unwired, unaddressed—supposedly sleeping. But he could not sleep yet. He could not rest because some untamed part of his mind was replaying the input data at threshold levels. Only bits and pieces. Snatches of conversation that had filtered down between the cracks, among the fissures and convolutions. Intersticed among the sirens and the smoke and the cries of men. Lucas grasped for the words as they scuttled like water bugs across the surface of his mind: "... of the experiment ... projected success probability listed as 96.73 if all variables remain ... must be injected at all levels in order to be ... most important of which is control ... unification of the spirit and ... the City is very ... dedication ... love ... control ... harmony is ..."

There was a soft Shield-glow seeping in the bedroom window as Lucas entered the room. Objects were gently accented in the faint illumination only suggesting their actual shapes to Lucas as his eyes danced over the half-seen things. He undressed slowly and then walked about the room touching the objects: twentieth-century hydrants, call boxes from the same era, carefully coiled hoses capped by brightly polished nozzles, an obsolete turn-out rig now hung upon the wall.

Lucas stopped fondling the things and turned to regard his wife, Delena, who was lying spread-eagled upon their bed, attached to the machine. He fitted the helmet to his head and clicked shut the visor; he stepped into his boots, feeling the heavy but secure grip about his feet and ankles. Approaching the bed, Lucas reached out to touch his wife, and he felt her warmth and wetness. She touched his helmet, kissed the smoked-glass faceplate, sending slivers of fire through his body. He could hear the crackling voice of the beast within his head, he smelled its smoky breath. Delena pulled him down and he came willingly into her.

There was never enough to make sense. Only enough to tantalize and confuse. There would be no unraveling of the puzzle. In that way lurked madness, he was sure. Better to forget. To accept. And sink beneath the comforting waves of exhaustion.

There was often a desire to share his joys with his men, but Lucas knew that the time had not yet come for such things. He was content knowing that he and Delena had been indeed fortunate to be selected by Chicago's computers.

And he was not swayed from this belief even after his worst fears were realized. There had been no anticipating the disaster; it simply happened. Lucas and his battalion were engaged in a fierce battle with a beast in a warehouse. The fire had started in the old building during the night, there had been no modern detection devices nearby because of the structure's age, and so the flames were monstrous by the time of Lucas' arrival. Some of the tongues leapt into the monitoring station of one of the generators which supplied power to the Shields—the outer protective shell of Chicago itself. Lucas was helpless in the face of the blast, the exploding generator, as pieces of shrapnel ripped into his body. Even though injured, he was overwhelmed by the brilliance and the heat; he ejaculated before losing consciousness.

When they discovered the panty-hose, Enforcement was notified. Lucas was transferred to the medicsector at Chicago's newly completed O.T. Complex. When Lucas regained consciousness, he was calmed by the reassuringly familiar environment. They treated his wounds and his Therapist discussed the incident with a delicateness that made Lucas very happy. The Therapist was, in fact, quite pleased with Lucas' imaginative addition to the process. Others came and spoke with him. There is nothing to worry about, they said to him. Chicago has planned for every and all contingencies. The medics who discovered you will not reveal your condition. The medics will not be revealing anything, they said. Soon, they will all be like you.

And Lucas lay quietly in his bed, smiling. Often he thought wistfully of his gear and the pleasures which they symbolized.

It was so good to be a fireman, he thought.

If man does not learn from history, he is doomed to repeat it. This is a lesson that the City has learned well, and it has made provision to save itself from any contingency arising from man's folly. A new century dawns with a terrible light.

SIX

The sun crept slowly above the cloudy horizon, sending tentative shafts across the wasted plains of the Agricultural Preserve. The blackened, pitted husk of a great food-processor lay in a distant field, blocking off part of the dawn, its silhouette a still-life metaphor, the skeleton of a long-dead beast. The sky looked angry, as it always did now, whipped and punished by a wind that spread death over the earth.

This was the view that greeted Taggart each morning as he rose from the ashes of his life. He started a fire in the brick hearth, lifted a cast-iron pot from its beam, and opened the door which led into the cool dampness of the cellar. The crank moaned as he lowered a bucket into the well beneath the house. He often thought of how the covered well had probably been the largest factor in his survival—for all that his survival was worth, he owed it to this well. Bringing up the water, he filled the pot and set it over the wood fire. The morning's first task begun, he walked out into the hazy light, pausing beyond the doorway to the small A-frame house to look at the collection of graves just beyond the clutch of now desolate buildings.

One hundred eighty-two neat piles of rock. One hundred eighty-two burials, one hundred eighty-two bitter memories. Taggart walked among the cairns, stopping before one that was indistinguishable from all the others. "Good morning, Father," he said into the steady breeze that seemed to swallow up the words as quickly as he uttered them. "The well's holding up better than I thought. And I think I've found some food stores . . . over at Henley's place. It was beneath the mushroom cellar. He must have been holding out on us all those years." Taggart laughed once, feebly. "You'd be proud of me, Father. I've been salvaging parts from some of the old machines. Trying to make a generator. Make a windmill. You know, get some real power around here."

His voice trailed off, as if he were expecting a reply, while he searched frantically for something else to say. Every morning he started his day here, partly out of respect, partly as an excuse to hear a human voice, even if it was only his own. He shook his head, rubbed his eyes, and turned away from the evenly spaced, neat rows of graves. Death is a part of life, he kept telling himself.

But he had never realized just how much a part it was.

Taggart walked slowly back to his home. He was more than two meters tall, gray eyes, and a shock of long dark hair so oily and dirty that it hung about his face in thick cords. Although he was only twenty-two, his features were accented by seams and creases etched by the sun, the wind, his grief over the past. He looked both old and young, depending upon how the light and shadow played about his face.

Reaching the house, he checked the water, which was boiling furiously, then returned to the cellar where the canisters of preserves were stored in long dark wooden racks. He selected some sweet potatoes and some pears, then returned upstairs to the hearth of blood-red brick. After grinding up some herb leaves, he placed them in a strainer and poured a steaming mug of tea.

As he sat at a simple wooden table, spooning out the pears, his thoughts were drawn back to the terrible war. It had been almost a year since the last aircraft had broken into a flaming smile and slid down the sky, yet scarcely a day passed that Taggart did not recall some terrible memories of that time. The Armageddon that had been expected for so, so long had finally come. No one from the Preserve, and its quiet days of a prior age, knew what sparked the conflict. It just seemed that one morning the sky was filled with burning things: missiles, fireballs and mushroom clouds, lasers, aircraft. The series of thermonuclear strikes, retaliations, and second level saturations lasted a frighteningly short time. And then, like ants swarming up out of their mounds, the armies appeared. Occupation forces from the ravaged Enemy territories, Defense forces from North America, Urban Complex Militia, guerrillas, and finally small ragtag bands of non-aligned raiders. Men poured over the earth, raping it, cutting it, killing it; men ravaging each other like hungry rats in a cage. Almost as an afterthought, bacteriological weapons were unleashed into the already fouled air, swept like dark specters across the Trades, the Maritime Polars, the Equatorials, reaching every point on the globe. Death could take no holiday and within a year seven billion were dead.

Only the extremely charmed, the natural immunes, the mutants, survived the Darwinian sword that swept across the planet. One of them was Taggart, the one among the thousands in the Agricultural Preserve condemned to bury the others. He often wondered if he was, as the old stories and myths often had depicted, the Last Man on the Earth.

And then came that morning when he knew that he was not.

After cleaning up from the meager breakfast, Taggard walked out into the ruins of what had once been the Community Core of the Preserve. The sun was high in the grayness that was the sky, betraying its position by an occasional spoke of light which pierced the cloud cover. He reached the lean-to he had thrown together, the place where he had collected as many useful tools and pieces of equipment as he could. The tower for his windmill stood behind the slant-roofed shed, towering above the wreckage like a lone sentinel, a last monument to the ingenious works of men. Taggart carefully roped the main drive pinion gear to his

belt, slung a bag of tools around his neck, and
began the long climb up the central column
of the tower. He studied his workmanship as
he pulled himself up the ladder rungs. It was
a curious blend of skill and frustration, of
wood and steel, of parts and scrap. But it had
held together under two vicious sandstorms
and countless rains. Perhaps he would yet
generate power.

Reaching the platform at the top, he
paused to catch his breath and contemplate
the harsh terrain of his kingdom. To the
north, where the orchards had once spread in
military ranks and files, there was nothing
but cracked, red clay, where an occasional
piece of mutated scrub or sage clung tena-
ciously. To the east and west, where the
shimmering grains and verdant leaves had
checkerboarded the black soil, there was now
an ugly mass of lichens and tubers that had
knotted and strangled the earth like gnarled,
angry fists. From such a height, Taggart felt
removed from all the changed things, but the
view of the southern regions, where the
Preserve's community once laughed and
danced and sang and cried and loved and
even hated, that was the most terrible view.
Everything crushed or burned or twisted, left
to rot or corrode, everything dead, scored by
the wind and dust, picked over by the rat
packs of desperate men, until there was nothing left but the stinking corpses. It would
not matter how high Taggart climbed, he
could never escape the memories of that.

He swallowed the lump that was in his
throat, and bent to his work. He knew that

he should be welding the pinion gear to the
rotor shaft, but there was nothing left even so
crude as a torch. His forge could not be carried up to the platform, and so he would have
to be content with a simple bolt mechanism,
and hope that it would hold. The work went
slowly, and there were times—as always in
the tasks he assigned himself—that he dearly
wished for another set of hands, another person to hold a bar, to turn a bolt, to feather
a board. As he struggled with the final bolt, he
paused to flick perspiration off his brow, and
gave a casual glance out into the desiccated
plains.

There was something moving.

Out beyond the limits of clear vision, out
where the haze seemed to grasp everything in
a wavering grip, he saw a black speck slowly
growing larger.

It was unusual for an animal to wander
about alone in this fierce world of scarcity.
The pack instinct had been recently reinforced and loners were easy prey, quick
meals. Taggart massaged the wrench nervously between his fingers, watching the figure steadfastly approach the ruins of the
Preserve.

A minute passed and the only sound was
the wind keening through the vanes of the
rotor above his head. Another minute, and
Taggart knew that it was a man coming
toward his position. Another man! A chill
passed through him. To hear another human
voice again! To listen to the thoughts of
someone else, to hear his views of the world,
the world beyond his own little scratches in

the earth. The palms of his hand grew moist; the wrench felt slippery. There was a dryness in his throat.

From the height of the tower, he had a clear view of the man. The stranger wore a long, flowing garment, a cape of some sort, that flapped and billowed in the breeze. He wore a military helmet, although Taggart saw what seemed to be a long plume jutting from it, swaying and bouncing with each step. The man also pulled a small two-wheeled cart behind him, its rubber tires leaving thin lines in its wake. The cart was piled high with unidentifiable objects that were bulging out from beneath a piece of canvas hastily tied down with rope. His steps were slow and almost mincing at times, which suggested someone of advanced years, and this puzzled Taggart. There was *nothing* in the direction from which the stranger had come. Nothing but desolate, scarred earth. He must have walked a great distance. Taggart slowly stood and watched the man, who now was less than a hundred meters away; Taggart wondered whether or not the stranger had yet seen him.

Just as he was considering a shout of greeting, a wave of the hand, the man on the ground looked up slowly, like a bird of prey, as if he had known Taggart's position from the beginning. Stopping in front of the wagon, the man dropped the towbar and cupped both hands before his face. "Hello! Hello, up there! You don't plan to kill me, do you?"

Kill him! Taggart was stunned by the

words. He had never imagined such a greeting. Hesitantly, he heard himself reply: "No, no, of course not! You're welcome here!" He stood against the platform railing, replacing the wrench to his tool pouch. "Here, wait! Wait till I can get down." God, it felt strange to be talking to someone again.

The stranger put a finger to the brim of his helmet, gave a grandiose, sweeping bow, stood up smiling broadly. As Taggart climbed down the tower, the man picked up the bar and started pulling his cart toward the base of the windmill. The stranger's words lingered in Taggart's mind. Why this talk of killing? Was the old man trying to put him off guard? Maybe it was the stranger who was planning the killing. Taggart paused for a moment, still several meters from the ground. No, it was unfair to get suspicious so quickly. Perhaps he should be wary of the old man, but certainly nothing more.

Dropping to the earth, Taggart dusted his hands nervously on his pants, and watched the man draw close to him. At the little distance that separated them, Taggart was able to study his feaures in great detail. The stranger's face was indeed quite old. Older in fact than anyone Taggart had ever seen. It was as if the stranger had never taken any geron-treatments. Beneath the rim of the helmet, a few wisps of silver-white hair danced upon a seamed forehead. Great bushy, white eyebrows huddled over the man's sunken eyes—two black ball bearings that shone as if recently oiled. His nose was thick and long, bent noticeably to the left. The man's thin, colorless lips were almost lost amid a ragged, bleached-white beard several centimeters long, but hardly trimmed in any uniform fashion. His neck was like a turkey's, the flaccid skin upon it succumbing to the pull of gravity and becoming loose and pimply. And everywhere there were lines, deep grooves cut into the flesh, forming dried-out folds and pockets where the years were embedded. Taggart looked at the man's hands; they were skeletal. White, gnarly, the skin stretched tautly over the bones, yet still wrinkled by thick blue veins. The fingers moved like insect legs, in quick, jerky motions.

"Name's Peregrine," said the stranger, extending one of his spidery hands. "What's yours?"

"Taggart. Nice to meet you, sir." The man's hand felt dry, rough, hard.

"You alone out here?" The old man looked past him into the ruined vista of buildings and machinery.

Taggart nodded.

"What's that you was doing when I came up? Trying to fix it? What for? Not planning to go chasing it with a spear, are you?" The man threw back his head and laughed at what must have been some kind of private joke.

"Chase it with a spear?" Taggart was mystified.

"Ah, you wouldn't know, I guess. Forget it." Peregrine dropped the towbar and rubbed his hands together. "Look, I been walking a long way and I could sure use a drink of cold water. Got any?"

"Yes, back at the house. Let's go, and I'll get you some."

Peregrine laughed again, smiling through his wiry beard. "Now you're talking, son. Let's surely go!"

Taggart put away his tools and picked up his bag, pointing the way back to his A-frame. "Where have you come from, Mr. Peregrine?"

Taggart wanted to ask him why he had that long pink feather stuck on the side of his helmet, but was afraid to.

Peregrine started pulling the little cart along behind them. He smacked his lips and said, "Well, I come from a lot of places since the Big Shoot-out. Listen, son, you ever heard of King Hamlet?"

Taggart shook his head.

"Yeah, well, I been with the King, helping him straighten out a few problems with his kingdom. And then there was—say, what about Captain Ahab? Heard of him?"

"No, I'm sorry, I haven't."

"Well, I was with the captain for a whale, I mean a *while*. We was out hunting down this mutant creature that seemed to be bothering the people round his parts."

"People? You mean there's still lots of people left?" Taggart felt his pulse jump and a burning seemed to be starting at the back of his neck.

Peregrine stood up and waved his arms dramatically. "Why, hell yeah! Taggart, you just been sitting here on your ass while the rest of the world's picking itself up and getting going again. Why, I been on the move! I guess you never heard of the Red Queen either?"

Taggart shook his head, dumbfounded.

Peregrine danced a quick little step. "I figured as much. Well, I seen her, too. Strange little place she runs ..."

"Where is it?"

"Where? Oh, you probably never heard of it. Little town down in the lowlands way south of here. But never mind about that, boy. How much farther till we get that drink?"

Taggart pointed at the tumble of wood and aluminum up ahead. "Not too far. Listen, Mr. Peregrine, how'd you survive? All that moving around and all? How'd these other people make it?"

"I don't know. Immune, I guess. Same as you, right? I don't mean to say that I ain't seen a lot of people kicked off, 'cause I have."

"Kicked off?"

Peregrine stopped, grabbed himself by the throat in a grotesque pantomime, stuck out his tongue, rolled his eyes. "You know, dead."

"Oh," said Taggart, as if he were grasping some arcane truth. This was an odd character, this Peregrine. Taggart did not know what to make of him.

"Yeah, it was them bugs they let out. Plague. I guess us that didn't get it was just lucky."

Taggart stepped ahead and opened the door

to his shelter. Looking back, he said, "I figured that. It didn't take long for everybody to . . . die off out here." He paused and looked back at Peregrine's cart. "You have anything in there you want to bring in?"

"Naw, ain't nothing but a bunch of shit anyway," said the old man. "Besides, there ain't nobody around to bother it, right?" He threw back his head and cackled his unsettling laugh once again.

Taggart gave him a mug of water and offered him some pickled vegetables, which Peregrine accepted and spooned out with his fingers. He ate with abandon, with no discernible manners, and lots of noise. "Stuff's not bad," he said finally, wiping a rivulet of juice on the edge of his ragged sleeve. "Where's it come from?"

"It was one of the industries we did out here. The Preserves were fairly self-sufficient. We didn't really need the cities."

"What was you doing on that windmill when I came up? You like to sit up there or something?"

Taggart smiled. "No, I was putting gears on the shaft. Trying to get some electrical power."

Peregrine laughed.

"What's so funny?" Taggart felt insulted, although he did not know why.

"Why bother with that fool thing? Why not come along with me and we'll find all the power we need?"

"Power? Where?"

"Where I'm going, of course. To Oz," he

said triumphantly, waving his hand with a flourish.

"Oz? Where's that?"

"I figured you wouldn't have heard of it," said the old man with a crooked grin. "Well, it's like this. East of here there's this magical kingdom that's got started. It's a funny little place. Got all different types vying for control and all that. Forces of magic and science. Things like that. The whole shebang's run by this nice old fellow. Calls himself 'the Wizard.' "

Taggart had never heard of a place like that, and for the first time, he began to doubt the words of this strange old man. "I never heard of any place like that. What's a 'Wizard'?"

"That's a fellow who can control all sorts of forces. A Boss."

"How far east did you say this place is?"

"I didn't." Peregrine guffawed, slapping his knee.

"Well, how about telling me."

"Why, would you like to go with me?"

"Maybe," said Taggart, weighing the possibilities. It certainly was not much of a life scraping along in the ruins as he had been doing. "Does this Wizard have electricity?"

"Coming out of his ears!" cried Peregrine.

"What?!"

"Just an expression. I mean, yes, he's got plenty of it."

"Oh . . . well, what about food? Does he have plenty of food? And music? Do they have music?"

"Sure they got food," said Peregrine. "But

music? What's with the music? You like music?"

Taggart nodded. "We always had lots of music out here. I'd just about give anything to hear somebody sing, to hear someone play something on an autar."

"Oh, yeah, I see . . . well, of course, the Wizard's got music. I hear that he plays the stuff all the time."

"Really?"

Peregrine nodded. "But that's not all they got. I hear that the women in Oz are the most fantastic creatures on the whole planet!"

"Huh?"

Peregrine looked at him warily. "Yeah, you know, *women*. You remember what they are, don't you?"

Taggart smiled. "Oh, of course. I was just surprised to hear you mention it, that's all. I haven't thought about women in a long time. It got so I used to think that maybe there wasn't anybody else alive but me."

"Well, that's not true. Believe me. How about some more of them pickled beets?"

Taggart fetched another canister from the shelf, opened it, handed it to the old man, who greedily stuffed several into his mouth.

Taggart watched him in silence for a while, trying to piece together the odd parts that made up the stranger. It was so different, so *exciting* in a passive sort of way, just to be talking with another human being, that their conversation had almost been secondary. But in the silence that now ensued, other than the slipping, slurping noises of the old man eating, Taggart reviewed the content of

Peregrine's words more carefully. That there were others alive heartened him. That there were places where men had not only survived the war, but were actually living constructive communal lives rekindled a hope within that he had long thought dead.

"When will you be leaving?" he asked finally, as the old man threw the canister into the fireplace, lay back in his seat against the wall, and exhaled loudly as if planning to fall asleep.

"Well, I don't exactly know. I wasn't planning to find anybody here and was just planning to stay the night and move on. But since you're so hospitable and all that, I just might be persuaded to stay on for a day or so."

"Oh, I see. But what about Oz? Didn't you say you were going to Oz?"

"That's right."

"Well, how far is it from here? How long will it take you to get there?"

"Now I'm afraid you got me on that one, son. Seeing's how I never been there, I don't know. Course, I don't expect it would take more than a week's going on any account."

"You've never been there? The way you were talking, I thought you'd been there before."

"No, I haven't, but I talked to a lot of people that have and they all say such wonderful things about it that I figure I've just got to check it out for myself."

"I see. Well, if you're serious about me coming along, do you mind staying a few days until I can think about it?"

Peregrine brightened, smiled, sat up slightly. "Why sure! I'd be glad to stay a few days. I ain't on no schedule. What's a day one way or the other, right?"

Taggart smiled and took a sip of tea. The room seemed to become warmer as he sat, basking in the glow of another's presence—even an odorous, unmannerly old man like Peregrine. "All right then, Mr. Peregrine. You're welcome to everything that's here. You can sleep over there. I'll fix you up a place tonight, after supper. Right now, though, I think I want to finish that mill. Just in case I decide not to go with you, I want to have some power out here."

"Suit yourself, son. If you don't mind, I'm going to take a little snooze. It's been a long and weary road for me."

Peregrine slumped over on the floor and curled up like a scruffy old dog. Taggart smiled and washed out his mug. He banked the coals in the hearth, and returned outside to be greeted by the hazy sky of indifference.

Later that evening, after Taggart had prepared a large meal, Peregrine went out to his cart and carried in an armful of odd things. There was a small package of cards with numbers and symbols, plus a few with pictures of men and women on them. Peregrine was able to make these cards dance between his fingers very quickly and rearrange themselves into what appeared to be random positions. From this arrangement, he performed tricks that ranged from apparent telepathic ability to obvious sleight-of-hand exercises. Peregrine also knew many kinds of amusements to play with these cards, eventually teaching Taggart the games of poker, blackjack, and tunc. They played for canisters of preserved food, and before the evening was over Peregrine had a large mound of canisters stacked by his chair at the table.

But there were other diversions as well. Peregrine's cart was a veritable storehouse of forgotten pleasures from a civilization on its way to dusty death. There were holograms of people and places he had never seen. Exotic tobaccos, liquors, drugs, soaps, oils, essences, herbs, spices, books, tools, weapons that no longer worked, pieces of equipment that even Peregrine could not identify. All of these things he claimed were gifts from the various "famous" personages he claimed to have met in his travels. The fact that some of them were damaged, either broken or partially burned, was always explained away with some slippery explanation that Taggart was not able to grasp easily. Peregrine spoke with a smooth, fluid delivery that was almost too accommodating, too easy. It was as if the old man sometimes knew ahead of time what questions Taggart would put to him, so rapidly and thoroughly could he provide all-consuming answers. Still, throughout the evening, Taggart was wrapped in a somehow magical glow that came from passing the hours with another.

When the logs and scrap wood in the hearth finally burned low and the lamps sucked the last dregs of oil into their wicks, Taggart was reluctant to sleep. His mind was

racing from the day's events but his body
was straining to fight off fatigue. Within
several minutes of blowing out the lights and
securing the hearth, Taggart could hear the
bellows-like regularity of Peregrine's snor-
ing. It came through the darkness in rattling
wheezes that soon became painfully antici-
pated. But it was not the old man's breathing
that kept Taggart awake, but more what he
represented. The young man lay awake for
uncounted hours trying to order all that he
had been told that day, trying to fit everything into a logical frame of reference. Was it
possible that the Agricultural Preserve and the
passing armies and stragglers that he had first
encountered after the war were just flukes of
this particular territory? Was it true that
other parts of the continent still thrived and
carried on the business of civilization? Then
why was there no power in the subterranean
cables? Why no maser energy transmission
to the foodprocessors, to what was left of the
Communications Module? Why had no one
come from any of the urban complexes to
help rebuild the Preserves? If there were people, then they would surely need the Preserves to live.

But it could be as Peregrine said. That
men had grouped into smaller bands, formed
little principalities, little "kingdoms" as he
called them. Saw no need for the larger urban
complexes and the Preserve systems. After all,
wasn't that in effect what his own ancestors—the fliers—had originally done when
they fled the cities? Anything, Taggart con-
cluded, was possible in a world populated by

creatures as strange as men. And for the moment he seemed content enough merely to know that there were men enough to try anything.

Even a place called Oz.

The next day, Taggart completed the gearing on the windmill and was trying to piece together the belt-drive system he had devised to turn the armature of a large generator built from cannibalized machines and children's toys. Peregrine watched this operation intently, although he offered no assistance other than verbal assurances that Taggart was doing things properly. By afternoon, the sky began to scowl at them and whirlwind ghosts began to pirouette across the desiccated plains. The dust and dirt buffeted them as they fled into Taggart's shelter like rodents burrowing into their mounds.

Taggart kept a fire going as he listened to the latest of Peregrine's tales—this one about a wondrous warship called *The Nautilus* that had somehow escaped the holocaust and was spending its days sailing about the earth's oceans stopping every now and then to dispense favors upon the shoreline inhabitants. It seemed that the ship was commanded by a munificent benefactor of great compassion. Peregrine at one time had booked passage on *The Nautilus* and sailed from one coast of NorAm to the other.

"How come you didn't stay with Nemo?" asked Taggart as Peregrine's tale finally wound to an inconclusive finish.

"Why should I, when I hadn't been to Oz

yet?" said the old man with a lilt in his voice. "Everybody should see Oz at least once. The captain even told me that. Besides, the Wizard can help people. That's the biggest reason why people want to go there. He can do just about anything."

Taggart scoffed at this last remark and Peregrine stamped a foot on the wood floor. "It's true, goddammit! Look, you just name something that you want, and I'll bet the Wizard could give it to you."

"Why would he want to give me anything?"

" 'Cause he's the Wizard!" sputtered Peregrine. " 'Cause . . . that's his job!" He grinned, beaming with a glow of self-satisfaction.

Taggart was not sure he understood the reason the old man provided, but he seemed so smug and self-assured that Taggart felt that it must make sense. He paused, thinking of something that he might get from the Wizard.

"Could he teach me to make music?" asked Taggart abruptly.

"Hell, yeah! That's no big deal."

"Really? Could I learn to play the autar?"

"Autar! Hell, you could learn to play anything. Everything! Make music all the time, you could."

Taggart sat back in his chair, gazing unseeing into the ceiling rafters. Maybe he should go with Peregrine. It felt so good to be talking again, to be trading ideas, even to argue occasionally. In Oz, there would be thousands of people to meet, to enjoy, to despise, to love. And there would be music.

"You know, I've been thinking," said Taggart. "That maybe I'll go with you. To Oz, I mean."

Peregrine sat up, his furry eyebrows suddenly knotted up tight over his small eyes. "You will?"

"Yes, you've convinced me that there's nothing here for me. Nothing but loneliness and quiet. Nothing."

"You sure about this, son?"

"Yes, I think I am. We can leave whenever you're ready. But morning's okay with me. The storm'll be passed by then."

"Morning? Oh, sure. That'll be fine. Sure, son, we can leave right after sunup. Now, how about a little blackjack?"

"Right now? Don't you want to talk about leaving?"

"Plenty of time for that," said Peregrine. "If we're going to be leaving this place, we may's well get in a few hands with a roof over our heads 'fore we do." He reached into his baggy jacket pocket and produced a gilt-edged deck. "Deuces wild?"

Before Taggart could answer, the old man started dealing the cards.

The hours faded away like drifting smoke as they played. Neither man spoke, other than to bet his hand or exclaim upon the luck of the cards. Taggart wondered why the old man had become so strangely silent. There was a look in his black eyes that indicated Peregrine's thoughts were not on his game.

In the morning, Taggart visited the graves for the last time. The wind clutched at him with chilly fingers and he shivered as much from it as the mix of emotions that filled him. For the first time, he felt self-conscious about talking to the dead, and he attributed it to the dark hunched figure of Peregrine perched like a craggy bird of prey in the fields beyond the graves. Taggart doubted whether the old man could hear his words; still, he whispered his goodbyes to the little humps of rock.

Peregrine had been reluctant to part with some of his trinkets, even though it would be necessary to make room for some of Taggart's foodstocks, tools, and the projectile gun that he had garnered from a dead soldier during the occupations. But Peregrine insisted on bringing along the weapon. There were still half-crazed animals out there; some were mutations, and some still dying from the poisons. It was a lot easier to deal with the unexpected when you were protected, Peregrine had said. And so they loaded up the cart and began pulling it behind them on their trek into the east.

Within several hours they had passed the farthest boundaries of the Preserve and the blackened, blighted soil stretched out behind them like a table top. Up ahead, Taggart saw a cracked, gray ribbon intersecting their path. "That's one of the connecting arteries," he said, pointing to the deserted road.

"Where's it go?" Peregrine shaded his eyes from the high sun.

"North is another Preserve. Eventually it cuts east to the Botaneering Complex."

"The what?"

"It was where they conducted experiments on plant life. They had succeeded in cultivating all kinds of mutations. Actually designed their own vegetables. Just like people, I hear."

"Oh, yeah. I've heard about that kind of shit. Good riddance, I say." Peregrine hacked up a mouthful of phlegm and hurled it into the wind. "Damn bastards had to fool with everything. Couldn't leave nothing be. Even the plants."

"It might be easier if we stayed on the artery," said Taggart. "It heads east pretty soon and that's the direction you want to be going in, right?"

Peregrine nodded and they headed for the road. Taggart was pulling the cart behind him and he was grateful to drag the rig up over the shoulder of the roadway where the tires could roll smoothly. The old man seemed to be as fresh as when they had started, but Taggart was feeling pain and exhaustion in every muscle. His knees, the soles of his feet, his calves, everything seemed to be on fire. Occasionally he was forced to stop, complaining and exhausted, while Peregrine taunted him and suggested that maybe he should go back to his fruit cellar and stay there.

When they stopped at sundown, Taggart estimated that they had traveled perhaps one hundred kays. As he prepared a small fire, Peregrine sat on a flat rock playing with a two-sided disk attached to a string. The old man would whistle and sing to himself as he made the object roll up and down the string which he had attached to his index finger.

"What's Oz look like, anyway, Mr. Peregrine?"

Peregrine snapped his finger and the "yoyo," as he called it, jumped up into his palm. "Well, it's quite a place, son. They got these big roads running all around it and through it—kind of like that one, except that they're made of big yellow bricks."

"Really? That's odd."

"Not really. Kind of pretty, I hear. Anyway, there's castles all over the place and, of course, the Wizard's got the biggest one of all. Carnival tents and bazaars, merchants and artisans in their alfresco stands, a million smiling people crowd the big boulevards, singing and dancing, buying and selling. They have gardens that just kind of hang off the buildings, big terraces with every kind of flower in the world, statues and monuments all over the place. It's just wonderland, I tell you."

"How could there be any place like that?"

"What's the matter? Don't you believe me? You've believed me up till now." Peregrine's lips pushed into a pout.

"Mr. Peregrine, I didn't say I don't believe you. It's just that it's hard to see how so many people could get through the hell that went across this planet so easily. I saw whole armies of men dropped to their knees, thousands of kays of wheat burning so bright that it turned the night into day. They poured so much shit into the air that it used to glow in the dark. What I mean is, where'd these 'smiling people' *come* from? What kind of power does this Wizard have, anyway?"

Peregrine laughed. "I told you it was a kind of magic stuff. That's the thing, son. You got to *believe* in magic. Or it won't mean nothing to you."

Taggart turned away from him, began poking a stick in and out of the fire. The light danced over his features accentuating his disbelief.

"Then why'd you come with me?" said Peregrine, his lips trembling, his eyes glistening in the firelight.

"I came with you because I was so glad to be *with* somebody that I guess I was afraid to be alone anymore. I came with you because I was tired of living like some animal. You came along and told me that there're people all over the world living like kings. I didn't come with you because I wanted to believe in magic. Now talk sense!"

Peregrine sat just beyond the glow of the dying flames. His lips moved but no words were uttered. He mumbled to the darkness as he clenched his fists into tight knots. Slowly, his shoulders slumped, his head bowed.

Looking at him, Taggart wished he hadn't lashed out at him, crushed him like that. "I'm sorry," he said. "I didn't mean it. I guess I'm just tired. I—I haven't walked this far in a long time. I'm sore and I'm tired and I was taking it out on you, that's all."

Peregrine did not reply at first. He sat staring into the darkness, kneading one hand into the other. "Yes, you did," he said finally.

"You meant it. And I don't blame you. Sitting around all day listening to the crazy talk of an old fart like me . . ."

"It's *not* crazy talk. I'm *sorry*, I told you."

"Don't mean nothing to be sorry. Especially if you were right in saying what you said."

Taggart stared at the old man, a hunched tragic figure. "What do you mean—*right?*"

"Well," Peregrine rubbed his beard nervously. "I don't know . . . it's just that—Naw, I don't know what I'm saying. You got me upset, I guess."

Taggart got the impression that Peregrine wanted to say something, but for some reason was unable to do so. He watched the man fingering the buttons of his shirt, avoiding his gaze. He couldn't remember ever seeing someone as sad-looking as Peregrine sitting by the edge of the fire. "This is really dumb, you know," Taggart finally said. "Here we are, the only two people for probably hundreds of kays, and we're arguing with each other. Hurting each other. I don't think man will ever learn anything, you know that?"

Peregrine chuckled. "Yeah, that's the truth, ain't it? Look, son, I understand how you feel about this thing. You just got to take my word for it, that's all. Some things are hard to understand and you just got to take them on faith. The way I understand it, this Wizard fellow discovered a way to get by. He made it, but don't ask me how 'cause I don't really know."

Taggart studied Peregrine's face, a mass of creases and sags, and saw the sadness, the pleading, that was there. "All right, I think I understand what you mean," he said after a short pause. "I guess I'll just have to wait till we get to Oz."

Peregrine grinned and the sadness disappeared. "That's about the size of it, son." He stood up and stared into the night sky. "We better get some sleep, don't you think? Long day again tomorrow."

Taggart agreed and they rigged the small polyurethane tent that Peregrine had cached in the cart. Within seconds of crawling inside, the old man's breathing fell into a deep rhythmic pattern and suddenly Taggart was alone with his thoughts.

He dreamt of roads of yellow brick.

The morning arrived like an uninvited guest, the harsh, hazy sunlight an annoyance that would not go away. Taggart struggled out of the tent to find his body crosshatched with pain. His bones, his joints, the muscles in his thighs, his shoulders, his neck, all stiff, unyielding. Despite the sun, he felt chilled and cold and damp. Thoughts of the warm clutter of his home did little to encourage him as he started a fire and boiled water for tea.

After Peregrine arose, they ate, packed, and struck out along the artery which stretched endlessly ahead of them. The bleak, barren landscape never changed—a continuous swath of cracked earth, punctuated by an occasional thorny tangled bush, a stand of naked trees. Rolling hills seemed to disappear as they approached them. There was a stark, wasted aspect to the land: no color, no smell, nothing. And yet, as they walked along, dragging the cart, Taggart could almost sense that the land did not want them there. It was as if it had suffered enough indignity, and the presence of men only intensified the bitterness.

Still they walked on, pausing only to share a cup of warm water, saving their energy by remaining silent.

By afternoon they came upon the bones of a dead animal. It had probably been a rodent of some kind, although the skull had two small horn-like projections above each eye. Taggart thought that the formations might have been evidence of a new mutation in the species.

Walking only a short distance farther, they discovered another animal skeleton, bleached and picked clean of even its connecting tissue. And then another. And another. As they looked ahead, they saw that more carcasses were visible. Like little white coils of springs, the rib cages lay in a vast graveyard.

"What the hell is this?" said Taggart, pointing to the grisly remnants.

"I seen this kind of thing before," said Peregrine, nodding to himself. "We're heading into some kind of hot spot. Must be off that way." He pointed to the southeast.

"Radiation?" Taggart felt suddenly uneasy.

"Yep. Something around here took a nuke. Any of these critters that happened to wander through this area probably picked up enough rads to knock it out quick."

"But why just the bones? If the radiation's that bad, what could be coming along to eat the bodies? And even if they could eat, wouldn't the flesh be poisoned so bad that they'd die anyway?"

"You'd think so, wouldn't you?" Peregrine laughed. "Funny thing, but it seems like the lizards and the insects don't seem to be bothered much by all that plutonium and cesium."

"You're kidding."

"No I ain't. Everywhere I been I seen them lizards scuttling around. They might be mutating some, but they ain't dying. For all I know, they might be liking it, might be getting stronger from them rads. One fellow I met near the Pacific—they got lots of desert out that way, and *lots* of lizards—he says that maybe the reptiles are fixing to take over again. This fellow thinks that maybe the bombs and shit were just the catalyst to start them growing up big and terrible again. Just like the dineysores, you know?"

Taggart stood for a moment trying to imagine a world full of giant lizard-things, thriving on the radiation that killed billions, inheriting the earth. It was a chilling vision, and he struck it from his mind only with some difficulty.

"I don't think we should go any farther in this direction," said Taggart wanly.

"Hell, no!" Peregrine laughed. "But I wonder what it was out here that took such a load, huh?"

"Might have been the Botaneering Complex," said Taggart. "There were a lot of materials and supplies and important men there. It probably was some kind of strategic target."

"Yeah, well, we might's well forget about it, 'cause we ain't going to get near it, whatever it was." He paused and studied the sky. "Besides, if my bearings are right, we should be heading north just about now, anyway."

"Really, you got any idea how much farther?"

"Not exactly. But my nose says that we're getting pretty close."

"Your *nose*?"

"Just an expression. I mean, I have a feeling that it's not too much farther. Maybe a day at most."

They walked for another three hours in silence, angling away from the artery and the deadly ground-zero that it bisected. When they stopped, it was on a slight rise that overlooked a gently rolling terrain. Taggart started a fire from some scrubby bushes and wiry hedge that clung to the tough soil, while Peregrine struggled to get the lines of the bright orange tent taut and secure.

After their dinner, Taggart looked up into the now sunset sky. The stars had already started twinkling in the east.

But there was something else.

"Hey, what's that?" Taggart said to the old man, who was already rolling himself up in the tent.

"What's what?"

"I'm not sure, but look out there . . ." Taggart pointed into the northeast. "What's that light on the horizon?"

Peregrine rose to his knees, dusting off his baggy pants. He picked up his feathered helmet, seated it firmly on his head, stood up to study the sky.

With each passing minute the dying sun revealed more of the night, and the glow beyond the horizon grew stronger by contrast.

"Jeezuz, it's huge! Whatever it is!" said Peregrine.

"I can remember when the whole sky used to burn like that," said Taggart. "When the fighting was still going on, I thought it would always be like that."

"Naw, that ain't no radiation. Too intense. Too goddamned bright! Goddamn, I don't believe it myself."

"What do you mean?"

Peregrine laughed long and loudly, then giggled like a child. "That's a city! That's a city out there beyond them hills! Goddamned if it ain't Oz!"

"Oz?" said Taggart. "Are you sure?"

"What else can it be? Come on, son. We can't camp here tonight. We got to throw all this shit in the wagon and get going!"

Suddenly all the pain and exhaustion were forgotten, and Taggart felt the adolescent thrill of discovery recharging him, spurring him on.

They walked as quickly as they could, in spite of the black moonless night. But the sky shimmered with the lights of Oz diffused through the atmosphere. What a grand place it must be, thought Taggart, transforming the sky itself into a beacon. He could almost hear the music in the streets.

Without warning, Peregrine's voice cut through the night with a painful cry. "My leg! It's got my leg. Oh God, get it off!"

Taggart dropped the towbar, started tearing into the canvas cover of the cart, groping desperately for the gun. In the darkness he could vaguely see Peregrine's silhouette, jack-knifed, writhing, arms flailing wildly at some unseen thing by his leg.

Something hard struck Taggart's palm. The stock of the weapon. Hard. Smooth. He pulled it from beneath a pile of junk and ran toward Peregrine, who was now on the ground screaming, moaning.

"Get that sumbitch offa me! Jeezuz!"

Taggart saw a long cigar-shaped thing; there was a hint of jaws and teeth, sunk into the flesh of Peregrine's calf. Taggart swung the rifle over his head and brought it down hard on the animal. There was a sound like a stick wrapped in a wet towel being snapped.

"Still holding on, son! Get him off . . . Oh God, get him off . . ."

Taggart reached down and felt a pulpy mass, scales, a bony skull and moist jaws clamped like a vise on Peregrine's leg. He pried the lower mandible back and the thing fell away from the old man's ragged flesh.

"What is it? What was it?"

"Goddamned lizard. I don't know. They must hunt at night. Oh God, it hurts. My leg's on fire!"

"I better get some light, Mr. Peregrine. You're bleeding pretty bad."

Taggart started a small fire, and examined the wound in the flickering light. The bites were not deep, but they were extensive. Taggart dressed and bandaged the leg as best he could, then stretched the old man out in the tent. The thing that had attacked him was less than half a meter in length, but half of that was jaws and teeth, it seemed. It had thick scales and bands of color around its body, tiny little claws and a thick tail.

Taggart made some tea, then checked on the old man. His breathing was rough and irregular, his forehead hot as an iron, peppered with beads of perspiration. He tried to get Peregrine to sip the tea, but most if it ran down his chin into his matted beard.

"Mr. Peregrine, what's the matter with you? Can you hear me?"

"Yeah, I hear you," he said, each word clipped, forced.

"Well, what's the matter? You didn't lose that much blood."

"It ain't that. I think I got poison in me."

"What?" Taggart felt the muscles in his neck, his jaws, constrict.

"That damn critter must have venom. Pretty strong shit, I figure. From the way it's getting me."

"How do you feel? Can you drink this?"

"That won't help. I can feel that shit burning me up. I ain't going to make it."

"Don't say that."

"Why not? 'Strue."

Taggart reached out and took the old man's hand, squeezed it tightly. Peregrine's skin was hot, but covered with a film of clammy perspiration. His breathing grew more labored, shuddered, wracked him as he lay on his back. "You won't die. We're almost there. The Wizard can help you."

Peregrine tried to laugh, coughed instead, almost choking at the end of it. "Son, I *know* the Wizard can't help me."

"Why not?"

" 'Cause there ain't no Wizard."

Taggart was confused, hurt, angered. The poison must have been very fast, very deadly. It was affecting the old man's mind. He was out of his senses. "What do you mean, no Wizard? Of course there is."

"Ain't no place called Oz, either. No *Nautilus*. No King Hamlet, or none of that crap I told you about." Peregrine looked up at him through dull eyes. Slowly the lids slid shut.

"Then what's that shining up in the sky ahead of us?" Taggart squeezed the hand again.

"I don't know. But it ain't Oz."

"How can you be so sure?" Taggart felt for a pulse and saw that it was frighteningly weak. "Come on, I'm going to carry you. We got to get help."

Peregrine tried to protest, but Taggart lifted him up and slung him across his shoulders. The old man's ridiculous-looking helmet fell and rolled away from them.

The hours dragged past and Taggart stumbled and staggered across the dark plain. Occasionally he stopped to check the old man; each time his condition was worse than before. If only he could get to the Wizard!

Another hour passed and suddenly Taggart saw something breaking the edge of the horizon. Something solid, bright and blazing. It appeared to be the uppermost edge of an arc. He increased his pace, and with each step the vision grew more substantial.

It was a shimmering hemisphere of light, energy.

Taggart gently laid the old man down. Shaking him, he spoke. "Peregrine, look, we've found it. Look! Can you open your eyes?"

Peregrine moaned something unintelligible. His eyelids fluttered open, unseeing.

"It's part of a dome or something. See it? It's Oz, Peregrine, Oz."

The light of the dome was reflected in the old man's eyes. His bushy brows twitched once, his lips trembled. "It can't be ..." The voice was dry, hoarse.

"We're almost there. You're going to be all right," said Taggart, lying even to himself now.

"Leave me here," said Peregrine. "Let me die outside."

"Mr Peregrine—"

"No!" The word was urgent, desperate. "But listen ..."

Taggart waited as Peregrine struggled to finish the sentence. For a moment, he feared that he was already dead. Then Peregrine spoke again.

"... just in case I was right, tell them ... tell them that ... Dorothy sent you."

Taggart leaned forward as Peregrine's eyes slid shut. "What did you say? What? Who's Dorothy?"

Peregrine exhaled once, his shoulders slumped, his jaw sagged slightly, and Taggart was immediately reminded of the grim pantomime of death the old man had once given.

He buried the old man in the dry earth just as the sun was rising. The dawn overwhelmed the glow from the city and if the dome still burned, it was invisible in the bright sun. Although Taggart hardly knew the man, he felt a great sadness. It seemed so unfair for him to die so soon after giving Taggart new hope, new purpose. The old man's death somehow struck him as more unjust than any of the others—perhaps even his own father's—and that made him feel worse.

He left the cart by the gravesite, untouched, unspoiled, like the pharaohs with their barges in their tombs. Whatever was left of Peregrine lay tumbled under the canvas top, and Taggart could not bring himself to disturb it.

By evening, his journey was almost at an end. Before him lay the City of Oz—there could be no doubt now—and he wished that Peregrine had lived to see such grandeur. Beyond the haze of the force-field, he could make out the countless spires and towers of a great city. The buildings were interconnected at various levels by graceful ramps, seemingly unsupported. The complexity of the architecture, the forced beauty overwhelmed him. And everywhere there was light and implied motion.

The closer he came to the outermost edges of the City, the more evidence he saw of the terrible war that must have been fought here. The ground was ragged and scorched, covered with the pitted hulks of half-disintegrated fighting machines. An occasional skeleton, half buried in the windblown dust and debris. Craters and troughs, torn up by the final descents of fiery aircraft. The scene reached up to the very edge of the force-field itself.

Still Taggart pressed forward, not wanting to pause for either food or rest. So close now, he thought. So close. Except for the wind, whispering among the wreckage all about him, there was no sound. No music, he thought oddly. As he drew ever closer, he had the sensation of being watched, not by any particular person or thing, but rather by the City itself. It sat before him like a great faceless creature, and abruptly Taggart felt uneasy, almost threatened, for the first time since coming to this place. It was not so much the lingering smell of death about the place—for he had grown accustomed to death—but rather the odd quiet, sterile brightness of the City before him.

Something moved at the extreme limits of his peripheral vision.

Snapping his head to the left, he sought it out, but saw nothing. Then there came a sound. A clanking. Metal upon metal. Taggart wished now that he had violated Perc-

grine's possessions, that he had brought along
the gun.

There was movement again. A flash of
white light and heat.

And darkness.

He awoke in a small room, strapped to a
flat-cushioned platform. A bank of instruments half covered one of the white walls.
There was a man of indeterminate age standing over him. He was totally bald, not even
eyebrows, his skin pink and puffy like a
baby's, small pointy nose, blue eyes, tiny
mouth.

"Who are you?" said Taggart, struggling
against the restraints.

"I am Pell," said the man, apparently not
disposed to give additional information
unless asked.

"What happened to me? Why am I being
tied down like this?"

"I am told that you were captured outside
Chicago. An intruder."

"*Chicago*? This . . . isn't, this isn't Oz?"

"Oz? What is an Oz?" said Pell, turning to
adjust several of the instruments.

"Never mind," said Taggart, thinking immediately of what Peregrine had tried to tell
him. Thinking of what he now knew to be
the fantasies of an old man who had seen so
much terror that he had dealt with it in the
only way he could. "What're you going to do
with me?"

Pell turned and stared at him blankly,
coldly. "You show a high degree of develop-

ment. You will be used in one of Chicago's defender-series experiments."

"Experiments? What're you going to do to me?" Taggart jerked his wrists against the mesh bonds. "Who's in charge of this place? I want to talk to someone in charge!"

"That is impossible. Chicago is engaged in many activities. It already knows of your existence. That is enough."

"Chicago? What do you mean? If that's the City, I want to talk to the Complex Chairman. The Boss. Do you understand?"

"Do *you* understand?" said Pell. "Chicago is our Chair. The City is an AI."

AI stood for Artificial Intelligence, Taggart knew. It was more a state of being than a concrete thing. It was that indefinable essence, an almost alchemical *happening* that men had strived to create through the matrixing of computer modules. It had not been successfully achieved up until the war, at least Taggart had not known of it, isolated as life had been on the Preserve. Yet here, this Pell spoke of it as calmly as the setting of the sun.

"And what?" asked Taggart after a long pause, "is Chicago going to do with me?"

Pell looked at him. "If you must know ... you will be surgically altered. You will be conditioned as a defense system. The City must be maintained."

"I don't understand."

"You don't have to. Accept the fate chosen for you. And be strong."

A door opened and two other men entered, nearly identical to the one called Pell. Tag-

gart began screaming, letting all the fear, the
hate, grief, and pain blend into one tortured
cry that did not stop even as they wheeled
him out of the room and down a corridor
from which he would not return.

After a time, he did not know how long,
since he no longer thought in such terms, he
was crunching across the wasted landscape,
flexing his limbs, his weapons systems. His
new body performed beautifully during the
tests. He was a seamless shell of armor, many
centimeters thick, bristling with sensors and
inputs that rushed information to the colloidal braincase at the speed of light. His
treads churned up the dry soil and the delicate but strong suspension system absorbed
every movement, every jerk and jolt. Deep in
the center of his body the machines pumped
and pulsed, the machines that kept his brain
full of nutrients and oxygenated blood. He
was happy.

But every now and then, an odd *thought*—
an image sometimes, a concept, a word at
others—would come to him. And he would
struggle with it, trying to remember something, but never actually succeeding.

And outside the City, where Taggart
roamed, the soil turned to dust and the rocks
to sand and a great desert rose up to cover the
markers and the dead things.

And he never found out about Dorothy.

*The City does not entrust its safety to
any agency other than itself—no matter how
indirectly. The citizens are reeducated
and history is redefined according to this
dictum. Priorities are reassigned and the
City plans for every contingency.*

SEVEN

Peering into the scope of the weapon, Denek increased the magnification until the lead vehicle filled the sight. From his perch on the high-walled rock face, he had a clear view of the intruders.

"Computer," he said into his throat-mike.

There was a humming sound in his helmet as the small terminal on his backpack reacted: "Yes," said the sexless voice.

"Send this to Chicago: I've found the intruders, and I'm going to intercept. Also, check for any new orders."

"Very well," said the machine, as it clicked off the helmet channel. Several seconds passed as it communicated with the City. Denek waited, while watching the three machines advance deeper into the valley below him.

"Denek," the computer finally said. "Chicago confirms contact. Intercept. Confirm kill. And return. That is all."

Alone with his thoughts once more, he prepared to attack. Why do they keep coming? he wondered, as he drew a bead on the first trac. He rested his forearm and glove on the boulder and squeezed the trigger.

Bright blue light pulsed from his weapon streaking into the valley below. The first struck immediately in front of the vehicle, but the second lanced the dome like a needle piercing a soap bubble. His scope was filled with flame, so bright that Denek was forced to look away.

In that instant, the remaining tracs broke formation and rushed to the face of the cliff nearest him. Realizing their tactics, Denek jumped up and scurried along the ridge to get a better shot. As he stepped out into the open, the computer's voice crackled in his helmet: "I am picking up a sensor beam. It just passed over you. They have detected you on the first sweep."

He leaned back from the edge of the cliff as the words trailed off. He was wearing a man-amplification rig, giving him cat-like agility and the strength of many men. It was a series of steel rods and artificial joints, fitted to his body like an exoskeleton. The computer on his back was plugged into the man-amp rig. Myoelectric sensors picked up each movement and passed it along to the computer; the movements were then coordinated and amplified. Denek preferred the rig to any kind of vehicle; it was small and compact, the gloves were actually gauntlets with retractable tools and weapons, and it also contained bio-connectors which fed his body nutrients and drugs, keeping him ever alert and able to do battle.

An explosion pulverized the edge of the cliff where he had been standing. The convoy's armament was more sophisticated than he had imagined. He remembered the last intercept mission—three vehicles, no large armaments: it had been an easy kill.

Quickly he began scrambling over the rocks, looking like some sort of crustacean. Two more explosions ripped into the rock behind him as he scuttled away. He felt foolish, allowing himself to be discovered so easily. He had had the element of surprise, and lost it.

Several minutes passed as he climbed and leaped down the wall of the mesa. He hoped to circle around and engage the two tracs on the valley floor. He instructed the computer to continue monitoring for sensor sweeps and began to creep around the wall of the cliff.

The first vehicle was within one hundred meters of him when he entered the valley. He held up both gauntlets and fired. The pulses ripped into the vehicle, but seemed to be absorbed into it like smoke being sucked into a fan. They were using shields, absorbing the energy and converting it to additional power for the shield itself. Denek turned and ran from his position as the trac wheeled on its treads and started trundling after him. Its turbine engines emitted a high whine as it accelerated, kicking up rooster tails of the desert sand.

The man-amp rig picked up his movements and soon he was zigzagging across the sand at almost 80 kph. Laser pulses burst around him, vitrifying the sand into glazed pools. He had no shield and was terribly vulnerable in the open.

The second vehicle began circling around

to his left, and the two tracs attempted a pincer movement—each one slowly curving in to his center. As he ran, he retracted the lasers and extended a mortar. The only way to penetrate the shield was with a solid projectile. Reaching the far end of the valley, he leaped behind a pile of boulders, gaining several seconds of cover. He placed the mortar on automatic trajectory and let the computer select the azimuth. Agonizing seconds passed as the preparations were completed. He could hear the clanking of the machinery growing closer and closer, filling his helmet with the sounds of death.

His extended hand trembled as the shell was fired. As he exhaled, he heard the explosion, and he jumped out into the open and fired a quick pulse of energy into the stricken trac. It blossomed into orange death, spreading a pollen of twisted metal across the sand. Turning on the second machine, still farther away, he saw it quickly reversing its direction, heading for an outcropping of rock to his left. He knew immediately that they wished some cover of their own, and he used the time to reassess the situation.

Several minutes passed after the trac disappeared behind the rocks. Possibly the crew was getting out to hunt him on foot, trying to surround his position. He alerted the computer to the possibility and instructed it to enlarge the sensor sweep to include organics.

"Can you get a trajectory on that thing?" he asked as several more minutes passed in silence.

"Negative. The distance is too great."

"No organic readings?"

"Negative."

Just then the face of the cliff above him began to erupt under a barrage of fire. The trac laced the ledge above him with several shots and thousands of tons of rock started falling toward him. He leaped instinctively from his huddling place. An ordinary man would have been crushed before taking more than a few steps; but the man-amp rig responded and he cleared the cascade of rock by many meters.

Out in the open again, he drew new fire from the trac, which had wheeled out from its hiding place. Once again he had to run, accelerating, increasing the distance between himself and the slower machine. There was no opportunity to use the mortar on the run, so he retracted it and extended the lasers once more. Turning back over his shoulder he saw the trac several kilometers behind him; he had escaped. The wind sailed over him, sending grains of sand up to tick against his faceplate.

"Is it still coming?" he checked with the computer.

"Yes. But it seems to be falling back."

He continued his accelerated pace, wondering what the creatures in the tracs must be thinking of him. Surely they were amazed at his speed and power, realizing that they were fighting more than just a man. Denek smiled to himself at the thought.

When he had increased the distance to over five kilometers, he slowed and stopped to survey the surroundings. He had been forced out of the natural valley into a flat open stretch of desert. The trac behind him was now just a black speck shimmering in the hot atmosphere.

"The vehicle has stopped," the computer said.

"Stopped? You sure?"

"There is no movement."

Denek put the rig into a rest position. He flipped down the goggles and brought the trac into focus. It remained still; he could see no one. They were both out of range of each other, yet their movements were obvious to one another. The game of waiting began, and Denek was content to wait them out.

Minutes stretched into hours. The desert sun, never clearly visible through the thick, half-poisoned atmosphere, sank deeper into the gray mist near the horizon. Denek replaced lost nutrients and eliminated wastes from his body. He was refreshed and eager to continue the battle.

Night came, changing the colorless sand into a blue sea of stillness, and Denek switched to infrared as he continued to watch the vehicle. He wondered about the creatures inside it, plotting and figuring, wishing him destroyed.

He took an injection of sleep serum which rejuvenated him, even though he remained awake. His mind churned over the events of the day. He replayed the kills, smiling inwardly as he congratulated himself on his inventiveness and instinctive actions.

He wanted to finish this last one and return

home. He missed the protective shell of the City wrapped around him and the others like a great cocoon. It was incredible that anyone could wish to destroy Chicago. It was so unnatural to him, he could not understand.

What type of beings were intruders? The question emerged slowly in his simple brain. Never seen, they were only known as an invading force that occasionally appeared on Chicago's warning screens. Perhaps he would someday learn more about them.

But now he sat, waiting for one of their vehicles to make its move. He could not fail, or Chicago would be threatened. The computer continued to scan the area, ready to warn him of any movement. The night wore itself out and the dawn approached.

Which was when they chose to attack.

He stood up in the man-amp rig, flexing and testing the extensors and weapons modules.

"They have dropped off two of their number," said the computer as the trac sped toward him.

"Where're they headed?"

"Spreading out. To both sides of you."

"Watch them. I'm going to take on the trac first."

Before either of them were in range, the trac opened up with laser cannon and it was effective. The pulses of energy striking the sand in front of him threw up a screen of debris, obscuring his vision. He set up the mortar and programmed the computer to zero in as soon as it came within range. The laser pulses began to creep closer to him. He stood his ground, waiting.

Suddenly the mortar coughed out its first missile and he quickly reloaded and it fired again. The first one exploded to the right of the trac, but the second shell pierced the defensor shield, ripping the left tread to pieces. Helplessly spinning, the trac was an easy target. He extended his arm and fired three rapid bursts into it and it disappeared in a bright orange fireball.

He ran, dodging, and skipping toward the two intruders on foot, being wary of their weapons. The one closest to him opened up first, anticipating his movements.

One of the bursts burned past Denek, passing through the steel rods of the rig on his left forearm. The heat of the contact seared his skin, causing it to ripple like chicken flesh. Pain washed over his senses and his hand and wrist were inoperative. They were locked into the gauntlet of the rig and he could not move them. He had the computer inject him with something to block the pain.

Still running toward the intruder who had wounded him, he raised his good arm and fired. Several bursts missed before he cut him in half.

Seeing the fate of his companion, the other intruder pulled back and started running from Denek. He stood watching as the figure dove for cover behind the smoking husk of the vehicle. Denek fired a quick pulse of energy into the wreck and it exploded once more. In the midst of the shrapnel rain that followed, he saw the body of the intruder bouncing and rolling across the sand.

"Computer. Contact Chicago. Confirm kill. I'm coming back."

The computer hummed as it followed instructions. Denek rubbed an enzyme ointment over his burned forearm, being careful not to touch the still glowing tips of the steel rods.

Just as he was about to turn away from the wreckage, he noticed the last intruder move slightly. It was incredible that he could have survived the concussion, he thought, and he was impressed with the creature's toughness. He raised his weapon to finish him off, but stopped, as an odd thought struck him. He had never seen one of the intruders up close. No one ever had. The only thing he knew about them was that they were treacherous, murderous beings who would destroy the City if given the opportunity. Denek had learned everything he knew from Chicago, but now considered the chance to learn something for himself. Perhaps he would even be rewarded if he could discover something new about the intruders?

He lowered the weapon, then flipped down the telescopic goggles on his helmet. He saw the crumpled figure, weaponless, one hand grasping at the hot sand, attempting to move, but failing. An organic sweep by the computer indicated a low ebb of life forces. Denek flipped up the goggles and selected a slow jog, heading toward the body. He wondered what sort of creature he would find. Anticipating the worst, he kept his weapon

ready in case the computer's readings were
not wholly accurate.

As he stood over the figure, his shadow fell
across it, giving it a darker, more foreboding
appearance. Denek huddled down, extended
steel fingers, and grabbed the creature's shoulder, rolling it over, face upward.

It was human.

Young. Feminine. Denek drew back his
hand and stood up. Confused, almost disappointed that he didn't find something else, he
felt his hands shaking slightly within the
gauntlets. He had never imagined that they
would be like himself. Chicago had never
suggested that it may be so.

To him, the intruders had always been
faceless creatures attempting to destroy the
City. But now, something did not fit into
place. He turned over the alternatives, the
possibilities. There were things he wished to
know; he could not yet destroy the female.

He looked down at her again, noticing that
she was barely conscious, with several deep
cuts on one arm and shoulder. He tore off a
piece of her jumpsuit, wiping up the sand-
caked blood, and tying it over the arm. Her
face was light, unburned from the fierce sun,
there were several wisps of blond hair along
the edge of her helmet. Long eyelashes. Full
lips. Sharp features. Angular, giving her an
unusual quality of not being pretty, but
somehow attractive anyway.

Several minutes passed as he stared down at
her. His pulse quickened as he noticed her
eyelids move slightly. He shook her and her
lips parted as she gasped for breath.

"Where're you from?" he asked.

No answer.

Denek kicked her. "Speak. Where are you from?"

Keeping her eyes closed, wincing from the blow, she spoke slowly: "The City of Angels."

Denek laughed. "I want the truth ... there is only *one* City."

"I'm telling the truth." There was no fear in her voice nor in her expression as she opened her eyes to see Denek towering over her.

"Where is this 'City' you say you come from?"

"A long way from here. We rode for many days."

"There is only one City," Denek said confidently.

Neither spoke for several seconds before she asked: "Why do you want to kill us?"

"Because you're intruders," said Denek, almost laughing at the absurdity of her question.

" 'Intruders'? What do you mean?"

"You approach the City. That can't be done."

"We only wanted to contact your people and—"

"You wish to destroy us," said Denek sharply.

"No! That's not true."

"You're lying," he said, but somewhere in his simple mind, he was not so sure. She spoke with an inherent honesty in her voice.

"Look, I'm telling you ... all we wanted

to do was contact your City ... see how you had survived." Her voice grew stronger as she began to shake off the effects of the explosion. Denek marveled at her roughness, in spite of her frail appearance.

"Explain what you mean." His curiosity grew in spite of his instructions and training.

"There were stories ... legends, I guess, that there were other places like our own. Once in a while men went looking. They didn't find much, but the stories continued. Some of the parties that came out this way never returned, so we came to check it out."

Her words seemed to be true to him, at least the part about other groups of intruders. He knew this because it was he who had destroyed some of them.

"They were unarmed," she added.

This was also true. Denek remembered how easy it had been to pick them off. He nodded.

"You?" she questioned, noticing his affirmation.

"Yes. It's my duty. Chicago demands it."

"You sound like the City's alive," she smiled weakly.

"It *is*. Chicago tells us all we need to know."

She didn't answer, continuing to stare into his eyes. Her gaze was uncomfortable and he was forced to say more: "Chicago is the giver and taker of life. Without him, we are nothing."

"Like a god or something," she said softly. She paused, biting her lower lip. "Well, I see ... I'm sorry ... I didn't know all that. Forgive me, please."

Denek didn't understand her, especially the odd word she used: *forgive*. He almost asked her about it, but somehow he was intimidated by her. It was an odd feeling, since he could crush her skull beneath his steel glove in an instant. Yet he could sense the power, the assuredness within her.

Several minutes passed in silence before she spoke again: "What're you going to do with me?"

Her words jarred him. She was so direct, so open. "I . . . don't know. I have been ordered to kill . . . all of you."

She looked over to the burned-out trac. "Yes, I know. You're very efficient."

Her words would normally have been a great compliment, but somehow they sliced into him. The female was so utterly helpless and yet she was not. He could not kill her.

Seeds of uncertainty were sprouting within him.

"Perhaps Chicago would be interested in seeing you."

She smiled. "From what you've told me, I'm not so sure."

"Explain."

"Don't you think it's kind of funny that we can talk with each other?"

Denek considered the question, his slow mind churning over the words. If she was truly alien, how could he talk to her?

"That's simple," he said haltingly. "Your people ... they've learned our tongue ... to deceive us ... to lull—"

She laughed.

Denek understood her disarming reaction: "I'm wrong?"

"If we can't even get close to Chicago, how could we learn your tongue?"

She had a point, he thought. "Still, there must be a reason. Chicago would know."

"Oh, I'm sure he does ..." she said, grinning, looking more desirable than ever. "But I don't think he wants to tell *you*."

"What do you mean? Tell me."

And she did.

The desert burned away the hours as she recounted the recent history of her City. She told him of the olden times when the men who had built the cities had actually controlled them, of how the cities were once swollen with humanity and of how men fought among themselves, killing and maiming each other. She told him of the drugs, of how the men who controlled their City learned to control the men within it by pumping drugs and enzymes into the drinking water, releasing the spores into the contained atmosphere. She told him of how her ancestors had rebelled and overcome the controls, taking away the power of their City, returning control into the hands of men. Her City functioned to serve her; not the converse. Denek challenged her many times, seeking clarification of a word or an idea, but always she had the correct answers. Her logic was unassailable. Heresy, yes. But still he could not help but almost believe her.

He dressed her wounds and gave her some of his rations. She refused to use any of his drugs, saying that they were not part of her culture. He deferred, attempting to understand everything he could about her.

As night came, wrapping them in the sudden coolness of the blue sand, they huddled closer together. Their talk drifted away from the cities and the ideas and the laws by which they lived. Instead they talked about themselves. He told her of his years of training in the Information Retrieval Centers, of his service in the military, of his years of being alone. She told him of her own years, of freedom and of curiosity. She had been free to learn and love and live. Denek was aware of this freedom she spoke of; it permeated her entire being. Her speech was clear and precise. Each word seemed to be carefully selected, yet she spoke without hesitation.

He felt clumsy and awkward as he sat by her in his rig.

Later, they prepared to sleep, and he watched her take off her helmet, stretching out on the sand. Her long hair danced lightly in the breeze. He reached down and released the pins of his ankle joints in the rig until he was free of the device. She sat watching him in the darkness, silent and waiting.

"You aren't supposed to do that, are you? Remove it, I mean."

"No," he said. "I'm not."

"But you want me, don't you?" Her voice was calm and controlled as always.

He inwardly thanked her for broaching the subject. Although he had never lacked a particular kind of warrior élan for such things, he sensed that it might be different with her.

He nodded and moved toward her.

He noticed her bandages. "Can you?" he said, his voice oddly uneven and sounding alien to himself.

She smiled and nodded. Then, lying back, she took him.

When it was over, she slept; but Denek lay there looking up at the stars through night-mist. Their joining had been a strange thing to him. She was so different, so receptive to him, so full of movement. It was an odd, almost apocalyptic thing, their joining. The suddenness of it lingered in his mind.

Easing out of her arms, Denek quickly refitted the rig to his body. He still thought of her as he did this; but when he had locked the final joint-pins into place and felt the weight of the computer on his back, he remembered everything. Chicago. He should have been returning by this time. He hoped that the City had not tried to contact him while he had taken off the rig. These were his thoughts as he injected a sleep serum into his vein.

The heat of the awakening desert danced on his faceplate and he was awakened also. His eyes fell on her, still asleep, looking even more sensual than the night before. He stirred slightly and the rig picked up his attempted movements. The steel joint creaked and the sound awakened her. Opening her eyes, she looked up at him and smiled.

"Hello," she said.

Horror coursed through him as he felt his right arm point toward her even though he had not initiated it. He tried to fight the movement but the arm continued to straighten. Knee and pelvic joints locked so that he could not take a step; he was helpless as he watched the weapons module click forth from the gauntlet.

He screamed to warn her, but the bright beam had already swept over her, slicing through her skull. He continued screaming as the computer's voice hummed in his ear: "Denek . . . be silent."

He felt a slight twinge in his left arm as the rig injected a muscle relaxant into his tense body. Soon he stopped screaming, and his body went limp in the steel cage around him.

"Why?" he asked. His mouth felt dry and thickly coated. "Why'd you kill her?"

"I merely completed a mission that you were unable to do."

"But . . . I thought that . . ."

"No, Denek," the computer cut him off. "Chicago was aware of everything. You did wrong."

He waited for more, but the machine was strangely silent. Then the rig began to move once more. The elbow and knee joints reversed themselves and he fell over on his back. Knowing suddenly what was happening, he fought the slow, inexorable movements. "Why? Please tell me!"

"It is simple, Denek. You know too much."

And that was all.

The rig continued to move, and his legs and arms were bent back at horrible angles, tearing away the connective tissue. The pelvic and shoulder girdles bent closer together, shoving his helmet toward his stomach, and the snapping vertebrae made popping sounds. Ligaments tore, bones cracked, and internal organs collapsed as Denek screamed. But during the brief instances of sanity left to him, he thought he finally understood what she had meant ... until the darkness descended upon him.

The computer made one last organic sweep over the pulpy mass it now enclosed, and satisfied, turned itself off.

Outside, the Earth is restless. Continents slowly shift, as mountains decay, forests disappear, deserts creep, and new jungles bloom. New creatures huddle under rocks, suck in the changed atmosphere, and struggle to adapt. But there is still one wound that will not heal, will not be altered—the City remains.

EIGHT

The room had at one time been a foreman's office on a maintenance level beneath the City. The room was surrounded by catwalks, ducts, pipelines, cables, vents, and shafts—entangled in a complex matrix of angles and planes.

Szel knew that there were thousands of abandoned checkpoints and offices like the one in which he lived, buried and forgotten beneath the multi-leveled, tiered City. Having been a Class One in Architecture and Planning had given him access to much arcane data about Chicago—the location of the old foreman's shacks being among many others. In the years that he had been living outside the rule of Chicago, Szel had mapped out hundreds of passageways along the subterranean catwalks, ventilation shafts, and pipelines. In fact, of all the City's thousands of apostates, it was probably Szel who knew Chicago's underworld the best.

Although there was no official "leader" among the Citizens who had rebelled against the ironclad control of the City's Artificial Intelligence, many looked upon Szel as someone of authority. There were reasons for this.

He had been one of the first completely to reject the edicts and guidelines of life in the City. He had been a Class One, which meant that he was of superior intelligence, optimum adaptability, excellent physical characteristics; he had been part of the elite subculture of humans who served just below the level of the AI itself. He associated with administrators, analysts, planners, scientists.

Even before he had walked out of his conapt for the last time, never again to appear within the Hall of the Planners, Szel had been aware of inherent faults in the City. But he had no proof. Chicago's immense Information Retrieval Center had lain fallow for generations, since there were few Citizens of Class One status who had the ability to use its facilities, and far fewer Class Ones who even had the inclination to seek it out. And yet, it had always puzzled Szel that Chicago had sealed off entire banks of data, restricted the access to whatever knowledge was contained within the crystals and spools.

Szel was convinced that, despite the propaganda broadcast by Chicago and displayed throughout the City, humans had not always lived a regimented, totally controlled kind of existence. But it had been impossible to document with visual proof.

And so he had waited through the years, hoping to discover something that might lead him to the answers. Years ticked by as he scuttled about beneath the steel tiers of the City, surfacing only to steal things he needed to survive. Once he had stumbled upon a subterranean entrance to a warehouse foundation that had been paved over; the workmen had ignored the waste and ruin within. In the wreckage he found immense crates of *books*. He remembered the joy with which he had plundered the forgotten treasures. Titles seemed to glow along the book spines in the dim light of his torch: *The Lessons of History* by Will and Ariel Durant, *The Territorial Imperative* by Robert Ardrey, *The Varieties of Religious Experience* by William James, *Love's Body* by Norman O. Brown, *The Immense Journey* by Loren Eiseley, *The Human Use of Human Beings* by Norbert Wiener, *Being and Nothingness* by Jean-Paul Sartre, *The Phenomenon of Man* by Pierre Teilhard de Chardin, *The Politics of Experience* by R. D. Laing, *Moby Dick* by Herman Melville, *Martin Eden* by Jack London, *Report on Planet Three* by Arthur C. Clarke, *One Two Three ... Infinity* by George Gamow, *Deathbird Stories* by Harlan Ellison, *Essays* by Ralph Waldo Emerson ... practically every discipline represented.

The titles themselves had sounded inspiring to Szel, and he spent long silent months struggling through the contents. The books were the key that unlocked the puzzle for him. They had become closer to him than any humans ever had and he hoarded them away in his undercity lair like a miser. Stacks of musty books, monographs, papers, and notebooks surrounded his bed and desk. A forest of paper which insulated him from the insidious machinery which droned above his huddling place.

In time, though, Szel found himself

reaching out into the semi-darkness of the maintenance levels in search of some other individual who had also fled the softly sinister existence; someone to share his treasures with. Slowly, a network of outcasts grew up and spread itself evenly throughout the City's viscera like an innocuous virus waiting to mutate into a more powerful strain. They would spend their days meeting in small groups, talking and arguing like the old Socialist clubs of London's San Francisco, playing games like Irving's villagers in Sleepy Hollow, manufacturing necessities from scraps and scavenged parts like Defoe's Crusoe, battling their fears and paranoia like Raskolnikov.

And through all this time, Szel strove to find a way to reach the masses, to deliver the word to the untrained, semi-mindless majorities who slaved through their Assignments on shift after shift and then lost themselves to the Amusement Sectors until it was time to work once again. Szel's precious books would mean next to nothing to most of them, since their only reading experience was the digital messages that the City broadcast to them during their Assignments. None could imagine that somewhere there might *still* be other places where man lived. Other places where his evolution had not been brought to a shuddering halt centuries ago.

Almost all of his time was spent writing a history of the City, dating back as far as he could document it, taking special care to detail the events of recent centuries, to describe as fully as possible the tragic sequence which had led to the present bondage of Chicago's inhabitants. Even as Szel wrote he wondered if anyone, other than the select members of the Underground, would ever read his grim account.

And oddly, as with many significant events in history, when the catalyst appeared, Szel failed to recognize its implications.

It happened one morning at a construction site near Chicago's Shield perimeter. A workman wearing a man-amp rig, and engaged in the demolition of old buildings, unearthed an object called a "time capsule." It was an ellipsoid less than three meters in length, just over two meters at its greatest diameter. Quite small in the relative scale of things, but it proved to be a most significant, most powerful influence on the lives of Chicago's Citizens.

The smooth lines of the capsule were broken by a corroded, pitted plaque upon which an inscription had been etched: *1976 Bicentennial Celebration, Chicago, Illinois. This Is The Way We Were*. When the workmen cracked open the still-sealed artifact, they uncovered wondrous, mysterious, revealing objects. A long list of City, County and State officials, prominently headed by the Mayor; a highly detailed map of the City accompanied by aerial photographs. A scale model of an architectural wonder of that era known as "Big Buck," and a portfolio of planned architectural structures, including a central computer complex, which would consolidate City services. A film entitled *Two Hundred Years of Progress* showing the evolution of American culture, and a Bell & Howell 16mm Autoload projector. Videotapes containing capsule news documentaries from July 4, 1976; a baffling drama entitled *Mary Hartman, Mary Hartman*; footage from something called "the Super Bowl." A Sony Betamax videotape play/record deck and television monitor. Cassette tapes of the Chicago Symphony Orchestra, conducted by Fritz Reiner, playing Charles Ives; major speeches by officeholders of the "Democratic party," greetings from His Honor, the Mayor, and a Bell & Howell stereo cassette player. A can of Hamm's beer, a bottle of Neo-Synephrine nose drops, a package of Armour Star smoked sausage, a "hero" submarine sandwich sealed in a block of clear Lucite, a baseball glove autographed by Ernie Banks, a pizza pie box autographed by Ron Santo, a Veg-O-Matic Kitchen Helper that still really worked, a Polaroid SX-70 camera, a Western Electric Touch-Tone Princess Phone, a Marshall Field electric-blue bikini, copies of *The Chicago Tribune*—"The World's Greatest Newspaper," *The Chicago Daily News, The Chicago Sun-Times*, and a Sears, Roebuck and Company mail-order catalogue. A complete set of Topps bubblegum baseball cards portraying the Chicago Cubs and White Sox, a box of Franken Berry breakfast cereal, ten handwritten tributes to the Bicentennial Celebration from Chicago public school sixth-grade students, a Batman and Robin Bat-Cave Gift Set, the November 1976, issue of *Playboy* magazine, the July 4, 1976, issue of *Time* magazine, the 50th Anniversary issue of *Amazing Stories*, a large folio-sized book called *The Best of Life*, and a family photo album belonging to Richard J. Daley.

At last, thought Szel, here was proof to the masses that there had been, if not a better way of life, at least a different one. News of the discovery, and the objects themselves, spread throughout Chicago like wildfire. Objects from the lost culture were circulated throughout the City faster than the authorities could round them up. Chicago broadcast official announcements condemning the "false artifacts" (as they were branded), and this only served to heighten the interest in the time capsule's contents.

Spurred on by the serendipitous event, Szel and his network of Underground fugitives launched a propaganda and information campaign designed to educate the masses. Teams stole through the artificial nights into the cybernetic complexes, the communications modules, the hologram stations and keyed in pirate programs and displays.

One program, which was subsequently broadcast through every con-apt holovision receiver in Chicago, explained in exquisite detail the society in which the Bicentennial took place.

Another explained the identities and functions of the mysterious Batman and Robin.

Posters which magically appeared overnight on every intersection displayed exquisitely how the bikini had been worn.

Another demonstrated the use of Neo-Synephrine nose drops.

A general communications bulletin blinked

across every Citizen's con-apt terminal explaining the game of baseball.

Charles Ives was rediscovered, and soon forgotten.

Baseball cards were flipped once again.

Someone had a Hamm's after untold centuries of aging.

A Polaroid picture was developed.

Patti McGuire lived.

Chicago, needless to say, was very upset about it all. The attendance at the Entertainment Sectors had dropped off drastically, work schedules fell far off the normal pace. Assignments were ignored. The totally controlled, perfectly ordered movements and operations of the City were suddenly in relative chaos. The Information Retrieval Center was practically stormed overnight by keyed-in requests for data on the "mythological" place called America. Chicago did the only thing it could do: it denied the requests and the existence of any such place or time. Flying in the face of such palpable evidence was the only logical defense for the great, thinking City. If it pandered to the whims of its inhabitants, the entire *purpose* of the City would be lost. If the schedules were not kept, if the functions and operations were not performed, then Chicago was failing to fulfill its age-old obligations. And since Chicago was a perfectly reasoning, perfectly functioning entity, it was incapable of failure. Therefore, denial of the distracting influences was a major priority—along with several others, which included *removing* the distractions. Those Citizens who persisted in toying with artifacts, badgering the Information Retrieval Center with foolish requests, promulgating unrest by interrupting cybernetic programs, tampering with crystal databanks, spools, and broadcasts would be punished.

The punishment, of course, being death.

As Szel recorded this last fact in his notebook—now swelled to several hundred pages of cramped writing, there was a knock at the door to the foreman's cubicle.

"Come in," said Szel, knowing that the City would not have afforded the courtesy of a knock.

The door opened and a tall, youngish man appeared in the frame. His face was obscured by a large brown beard so that the only prominent feature was his bright blue eyes. He wore the drab green coveralls of a Class Four laborer, but it was obvious from his expression and his posture that he was not one of those genetic defectives.

"Gabe," said Szel, recognizing his friend. "Sit down if you can find some space. What's been going on out there?"

"It's getting bad," said the tall man as he pushed a pile of books to the side, easing down to the floor. "Chicago broadcast more executions today. Ten thousand and some odd. I can't believe it."

"How are the people taking it?"

"That's the most incredible part. They're not knuckling under like Obie thought they would. They're *doing* things."

Szel laid down his pen, rubbed his aching fingers together. "Such as . . . ?"

"Such as there's a hell of a riot going on up on Level Three right now. There must be a couple of hundred thousand workers—mostly Threes and Fours, I guess—they've jammed up the streets. Traffic backing up, plowing into the crowds . . . it's bad."

"What started it?"

"Not sure. It could have been the broadcast of the executions, but it could have been something smaller. I heard some of the people talking about Chicago threatening to shut off the water supplies to the Unit Assembly Workers unless they returned to previous production and maintenance schedules. There was a lot of noise about that, and some of the Workers started walking out of the Assembly Works."

"That's never happened before!" said Szel.

"It's especially ironic that the whole thing's happening at the Unit Assembly Plant, don't you think? Those things are Chicago's latest project, and I've heard talk that the City will start using them to control the crowds if things get much worse."

Szel shook his head. "That would be very bad for our side." He imagined for a moment the packed avenues of people swarming away in panic from the tall, strong robots.

"Listen, I was just with Obie. We were in one of the maintenance shafts that runs up through the Shield Generators. The thing with the Assembly Workers looks like it's only the beginning."

"What do you mean?"

"The police have been instructed to arrest some Citizens dressed up like Batman and Robin. Whoever they are, they've been running around the top levels sabotaging equipment, cutting transmission cables, things like that."

Szel laughed. "Batman and Robin! That's fantastic! Look what we've started, huh?"

"Obie and Vagas think that we should get in touch with as many Undergrounds as we can. They think we should start intensifying the propaganda campaign."

Szel nodded. "This is better than our wildest dreams, Gabe! The people are ripe for something ... Think of it, after all this time, all this immeasurable time, mankind standing up on its hind legs again, standing up to fight for what it really wants."

"Do you really think they can do it?"

"They've got to want to do it. They've got to want to do it more than anything else in their lives. They've got to want it more than the drugs and the brain-stims, more than anything." Szel got up and walked to a stack of books in the corner of the room. He shuffled through them, finding the title he wanted, then quickly thumbed through its pages. "I can remember the first time I read these lines," he said, marking a spot in the book. "I sat there realizing that I was probably the first human to be reading them in aeons, and I felt a chill run through me like a knife blade. The lines seemed to jump out at me from the page: *'As if you could kill time without injuring eternity. The mass of men lead lives of quiet desperation. What is called*

*resignation is confirmed desperation. There
is no play in them for this comes after work.
But it is a characteristic of wisdom not to do
desperate things.'* "

Szel closed the book slowly, shaking his
head. "If only they could have found
Thoreau instead of Batman."

"No," said Gabe, smiling. "If they'd
found Thoreau, they wouldn't have done a
thing. Better Batman than nothing at all."

"Yes, you're right. I know you're right,
but I can still be an idealist, can't I?"

"Yes, I guess you can." Gabe walked past
the older man and looked down at the open
notebook on his desk. "How's the notes coming along?"

"Coming, as usual. And now, it may be
even more important than I first imagined.
If these riots ever turn into a full-scale
revolt, if we can bring down the rule of the
AI, the survivors will need something to
build upon." Szel picked up the notebook,
holding it up before him in both hands.
"They will need something like this!"

Gabe nodded, and turned to leave.

"Where're you going?" asked Szel.

"I've got to go up top. Don't you want to
know what's going to happen with the Assembly Workers?"

"Oh, yes, of course." He paused. "I'm
sorry if I scared you off with all that grandiose talk."

Gabe shook his head as he stood by the
door. "You didn't scare me off. I really do
have to get going, that's all."

"No, I know I must sound a bit crazy . . .

Sometimes we get so wrapped up in what we're doing that we forget ... we forget that there are others involved. I'm sorry."

Gabe walked back and touched Szel's shoulder, smiled, then turned to disappear beyond the door and down the maze of catwalks.

Szel returned to his desk and prepared to outline the most recent incidents for inclusion in the historical gestalt of Chicago. As he sat crimping the pen between his fingers, he replayed the exchange with Gabe. Szel did believe what he had told the man. After all, no one else was dedicated to the task of preserving what had happened. No one else was ensuring that the same mistake never happen again, that mankind never allow itself to be served so well. What was it that Thoreau had written about men choosing the sterile life? He said it was because they truly believed that there was no other choice. That is precisely what Chicago had instilled in his generations of the trapped, the controlled.

Yes, he was right, thought Szel, as he continued to write.

And while Szel worked, carnage reigned many levels above his head. The riot among the Assembly Workers continued through the time for a change of shifts. The mob, which had grown to monstrous proportions, seethed and surged through the wide avenues, acting with the group-mind that governs such entities. And through this mass of moving flesh waded the Brobdingnagian figures of Chicago's Units. Towering caricatures of men, their alloyed bodies gleaming in the light of the fires, their long spindly legs scissoring into the crowds, their finely articulated hands sweeping, tearing, mincing the unfortunate bodies in the robots' course.

Into this mayhem flowed hundreds of thousands of Citizens just released from their Assignments.

All this was registered and recorded and transmitted to the Central Databanks of Chicago. Routings and subroutings were disrupted as the immense machine-construct sought a logical solution to the illogical problem. It accessed its boundless memories, relays clicking furiously, chips and processors glowing like hot steel with the light-speed rush of data pulsing through them. Contingencies produced, analyzed, chosen or discarded in the flick of an eye. The City sought to rid itself of the cancer which grew within.

Enforcement squadrons, firemen, perimeter defensemen, sentries, the Units, everything was thrown against the insurrection. Chicago's orders were direct, simple, succinct: eliminate the offenders.

And so, wrote Szel, a quarter of a million died that day.

It had been the declaration of war. Despite the efforts of Chicago to keep the news of the massacre from spreading to the other Sectors of the City, the horror of Level Three was on the lips of everyone—from the lowest Class Fives up to the Administrators and the Analysts.

Entire shifts refused to show up at their Assignments. The production of vital materials—such as recycled foodstuffs, water, oxygen, electrical power, fuel cells—slowed almost to a halt. Chicago retaliated by sealing off some of the lower Levels and Sectors—effectively suffocating and/or starving thousands. Battles raged through the artificial nights and into the clockwork days until the man-amped Police and Sentries were either overwhelmed or threw off their rigs to join their brothers in the rebellion.

And then it became a more coldly defined thing. Something more simply described: man against machine.

The madness continued as millions were cut off from their drugs, their stimulants, their air and sustenance. Driven like crazed, caged beasts, they swarmed over the sterile tiers and Levels of the City, either to destroy or be destroyed, it mattered little to them.

And so it did not really surprise Szel when Gabe and Obie came for him.

"Are you sure we must leave?" he said, needing the reinforcement anyway.

"The mobs are being driven down into the lower Levels. They're trying to sabotage the fusion reactors and the geothermal turbines. They'll be passing right through here eventually."

"But where can we go?" Szel stood and quickly surveyed the room—his home for so many years—knowing that he would probably never see it again.

"We're going to try and make it to the Outside," said Obie, a short, dark-complected woman with closely cropped hair.

"*Outside*? How?"

"Chicago's shut off the Shields on the Southern Perimeter. The robots are herding as many of the mobs as possible out through the Generator Gates. It's either that or stay here and be trapped."

Szel's mind reeled with the suddenness of the information. It was like the news of an unexpected death. For a moment, the mind seems to seize up, unable to process the data, unable to accept what it receives. Or like finally realizing that an enemy has been defeated, and recognizing the void that would come from the absence of a nemesis. To be free of the City's bondage was a dream Szel had tendered for so many long years, and now that the moment was at hand, a part of him wanted it to remain a dream.

"How much can we take with us?" he asked after a long pause.

"Not much," said Gabe, gazing quickly about the room. "We're going to have to move pretty fast. Some of the others, from 112-B and 98-A, have already left."

Szel looked at the pieces of his life scattered about the small quarters. How could he *choose?* There was no time to mull over this title or that, no time to balance Melville against Russell. "I can't," he said. "It's impossible! We can't leave everything to be destroyed! Not after all this!"

"You can stay if you want," said Obie. "But none of this will do you much good dead."

Szel quickly manufactured a rationalization. If these books had survived, then surely *somewhere* on the planet there were other copies that had escaped oblivion. And surely, Chicago retained datalogues somewhere within its restricted areas at Information Retrieval. Better stagger away from Babylon with a full belly anyway, he thought. "All right then. Just a few things we might really need . . . and *this*," he said, reaching for his notebook.

Gabe nodded approval and helped him stuff some clothing and rations into a backpack.

When they reached the maze of catwalks, Szel took the lead. They entered a ventilation duct and followed Szel's torchlight down the smooth silent corridors, safe for the moment from the death that was swarming into the maintenance Levels.

As he walked, Szel carried the notebook—the history and the warning to the future generations—close to his chest, wrapping it tightly in his jacket. If there was one thing he must preserve, it was the notebook. Once free of this place, he thought, he would have to father a son—something he had vowed never to do as long as he lived under the shroud of the AI. He would teach his son, and his son would teach others, and a new race of enlightened men would grow up to pass along the terrible truths that he had endured.

After a time, they came to an intersection of three ducts. Beyond the thin metallic walls of the ventilation chambers, all three could hear the indistinct murmurings of a great many voices, the clatter of footsteps along the steel walkways. Szel paused for a second, listening, mapping out a route, then selected the middle shaft, which gradually curved up and away from the descending masses.

They came at last to a vertical shaft, conveniently lined with a ladder which rose up to a dark vanishing point. They climbed in darkness, passing numerous intersecting horizontals, until they reached the one which Szel knew, from long years of exploration, would lead to the Southern Perimeter.

When they reached it, it was night Outside. Coming up in a building adjacent to one of the large Shield Generators, Szel was shocked to see the absence of the bristling, coruscating radiance of Chicago's force-field. But there was no time for abstract observations; they had emerged into the middle of a nightmare scene. Below the platform where they stood was an ocean of bodies streaming headlong through the huge arches that formed the bipolar gates of the Shield Generators. Behind them were the stalking shapes of the Units, holding large subsonic weapons, unleashing invisible death upon the throng.

Gabe carefully guided the others down the side of the platform, staying close to the large structural supports which offered some protection from the swath of the Units' weapons. Reaching ground level, they joined the crush of bodies racing madly out of the City.

Szel looked up and saw a deep velvet-blue sky, streaked with hazy clouds, like wisps of smoke. Pushed along over the uneven terrain, he clutched at the straps of his pack and the

notebook tucked up under his right armpit.
Hands in the crowd tugged and pulled at him
and he swung his elbows wildly to keep them
away. His breath rushed in and out in cold
searing bursts and he could smell alien scents
from the Outside. Despite the atmosphere of
panic that surrounded him, he kept looking
skyward, searching for the faint specks of
starlight that occasionally pierced the thin
cloud cover. Ahead of him, he saw the tall,
bearded figure of Gabe, struggling to keep
him close in the mad crush of bodies that was
fanning out across the bleak landscape.

He closed the distance between himself
and his companions, his legs pumping automatically, without feeling, becoming like
rubber, his lungs burning. Oddly, the
crowd's density did not seem to be decreas-
ing, despite the growing distance it gained
from the perimeter of the City. There was
something especially frantic about the mob,
even though it was out of immediate danger.
The majority of the fleeing masses seemed to
be charged as if by an electrical current—a
feeling that approached hysteria. Szel felt it
himself, enveloping him like a dark cloak,
like some unseen specter.

And suddenly he knew what it was. It was
the fear of the open space: the sight of the
clouds and the boundless vault of the night
sky, the chill wind that swept through them
like invisible fingers, the stark emptiness that
enveloped them, forcing them to bunch and
press themselves together.

Agoraphobia it was called, Szel knew. But
naming his fear had little effect on dispelling

it. He heard someone scream very close to him, and, as if on cue, others took up the wailing until thousands of voices rose up as one, like a chorus out of hell itself. Szel opened his mouth and screamed, trying to release the demon within. He stumbled in a depression in the earth. Falling, he pressed the notebook close to his chest.

When he awoke, the sky was bright and filled with a diffused hazy light. Gabe and someone he did not recognize were kneeling by his side; they were nestled in a bowl formed by the placement of several large rocks.

"You're safe now," said Gabe. "We're all safe."

"How?" said Szel. "The notebook!" His hands flew to his empty jacket.

"I've got it right here. Lucky I somehow got forced behind you out there. I saw you go down, got to you pretty fast."

"What about the City? The crowds?"

"They kept pouring out through most of the night. The part of it we were in drifted for hours. I kept you up on my shoulders. Not too bad really. The pressure of everybody around me helped. When the sun started to come up, the warmth and the light quieted them. Gradually, things slowed, thinned out."

"And the City?"

"Hard to tell, now. Who knows what's going on back there. It might be the end."

"The end?"

"Of man, I mean," Gabe said, tugging at

his beard. "I wouldn't be surprised if the City just doesn't clean out everybody."

"That's not exactly the way we planned it, is it?" Szel shook his head.

"We didn't really plan very much of it, did we?" Gabe smiled.

"No," said Szel as he reached out to hold his notebook. "But with this to keep us from forgetting, perhaps we can now."

He lay back, drawing a breath, thinking of what was to come.

It is a difficult thing to accept the inevitable, to recognize a problem and be unable to correct it. For the first time in its long history, the City feels the pain of loss—the loss of one's parent.

Beyond its barriers, Life abides as the centuries dissolve into one another. New species clamber to dominance as an old, familiar one declines.

NINE

The western sky was an open wound. The wind was cold and quick, quartering the wasted plain like a hungry wolf. Soon the sun would be lost in the darktime and still the tribe had nothing to eat. The old man they called Simrin thought about this. It was not good for them to travel all day and sleep with empty bellies. That meant weakness, death. Surely the gods would not be so cruel to his people, especially while they made their pilgrimage.

Simrin turned his ashen, wrinkled face toward the north where the hunting party had gone. He was being dragged along behind the others in a crude sled, lashed together with strips of lizard skin, for he was too weak and too old to walk. They would have left him to die, had it not been the winter solstice. In their kindness, they brought him so that he might pay respects at the Heart of the World one last time.

Still, the winter solstice, he thought, gripping the rotten pack tightly, pulling the pelts more closely about his sunken chest. It was odd that such a superstition should persist after all this time. Was it, perhaps, some racial

memory in man, dredged up from Druid
depths, that placed significance on the short-
est day of the year? Or was it—

A hoarse, croaking sound broke the evening silence.

It became a bellowing cry which reached
out for them in the semi-darkness. Louder.
Closer, thought Simrin; the hunters were now
the hunted. There would be meat this evening after all, although he did not yet know
for whom. Helpless but to watch, he waited
for the band of thirty odd—mostly women
and children—to gather together into a tight
circle, drawing Simrin's sled into the center
of the circular knot.

Three adolescents held their spears out like
the spokes of a wheel as they searched the encroaching darkness for the thing that cried
out for them. Suddenly there was the
scrutching of loose stones, footsteps approaching. Simrin turned his head and saw
the hunting party running toward them in
the half-crouches of the wary ones who survive. The darkness seemed to cling to them
and he could not see their faces, yet he knew
that fear would be found there. He wondered
how far behind them the beast now moved.

The hunters formed a spear-tipped rim
around the others, and Simrin, in the center
of the pack, could see nothing but the long
greasy hair of the backs of their heads. No
one spoke, not even the children uttered the
slightest whimper. In the outer darkness the
crunch of dry earth signaled the beast's approach, and the band could only wait.

Out of the twilight it came. A gray hulk,

shambling on four tree-trunk legs, a thick bony head with eyes that bulged like obscene blisters. Its movements were quick, instinctive, and its serrated jaws snapped and clicked like parts of a machine.

The hunters waited until it was so close that they could not miss. So close that even Simrin could hear the creature's breath coming in rapid, panting bursts. So close that the flickering tongue could almost touch them. Then, for an instant, the beast stopped, frozen, as if captured in a frame of film.

Someone screamed and the spell was shattered. The beast tensed to spring, the hunters plunged their spears into the gray mass. Its scream cut through the night like the rough-edged blades which slashed its body. It writhed and clawed furiously, blindly, backing up, lashing its tail like a whip, and the hunters pressed their advantage. Again and again they drove their stone-tipped weapons into the scaly flesh. The air was thick with the smell of blood and screaming.

Then, as suddenly as it had begun, it was over. Simrin heard the beast drop. A muffled concussion which shook the earth, a death-gasp rattled in its throat, and it was still. The children stood up cautiously, but anxious to see the dead beast; the women began to murmur as they stood and sought out their mates. Soon Simrin was alone in his sled, watching in the light of the rising moon as his tribe encircled the lizard excitedly to flay its skin and render its flesh. Soon the women would be sent out to gather kindling, one of the adolescents would strike the firestones, and the tribe would eat their fill.

Simrin lay listening to the language of his brothers and sisters as the divisions of labor were parceled out and the feast prepared. If he sat like this—objectively removed, like the participant observer of the ancient anthropology books—and listened to their speech, he was reminded of how much the language had changed. Or deteriorated. There were few complete sentences, no abstractions, no implied expressions, no figurative phrases, no idioms. Some of the slower members of the tribe seemed to make do with an odd assortment of grunts and guttural groans, which were lost upon Simrin. To see the group, clothed in animal skins cinched with simple thongs, unwashed, some deformed, most with advanced gum diseases, others with tumors, was a natural yet shocking sight. Simrin recalled his own childhood when there was a village by a large, muddy river. He remembered the houses made of sticks and dried mud bricks, the simple crops, the dancing and singing around community fires during the darktimes. Somehow, they had lost all that.

One of the children interrupted his tired memories—the oldest of which were far more lucid than the events of recent days—with a stick upon which a strip of smoking meat had been skewered. Simrin chewed the rough, fibrous piece, trying to ignore its pungent, gamy flavor, and thanked the boy. The child smiled and returned to his mother, leaving Simrin with thoughts of his own son—now dead for forty winters. He remembered the morning he found the small, pale body floating face down, still and cold, in the sky-blue pool among the rocks behind their hut. It was not unusual to lose children, even then, but Simrin had known that the loss of his child was more than a personal tragedy. Even in his youth, it had been growing more difficult to make women fertile, and something deep within his soul knew that there would be no other sons to him.

He was not alone in this curse, and as the years dragged by, the tribe's number declined, their skills dwindled. The horror of their descent, to Simrin at least, was that he was apparently the only member of the tribe to realize that their culture was flaking away like dry leaves in a persistent wind.

Finishing the strip of meat, Simrin cast down the blackened stick. He crossed his arms and felt the pack under his clothes. His father had given him the pack, and the Notebook within it, many winters ago on the night he had died. Simrin's father had received it from *his* father, who had also received it from *his* father—the man who had written the words upon the cracked, brown-edged pages. Simrin touched the pack, remembering the almost liturgical speech that his father had told him about the Notebook—how it was the key to keeping man safe from the evils of the serving machines. They were certainly safe from *that*, thought Simrin.

Some hunkered down by the fire and added more kindling and in a few minutes the light

flared and flapped more brightly. Simrin lay
back in his sled and opened the pack. Its
edges were worn down to the intricate stitch-
ing, the straps which once allowed it to be
worn on one's back were either broken or
worn through. The Notebook itself was not
in much better condition. The hidebound
cover was split and cracked along the spine,
wrinkled and stained across both front and
back flaps. The paper was brittle, discolored;
the ink faded and in some places blurred
from previous moisture. Yet the majority of
the text was still readable, and just looking
at the pages brought back entire scenes from
Simrin's childhood. He could close his eyes
and see his father unpacking the Notebook
and placing it before his son, slowly pointing
to each letter, pronouncing it, redrawing,
giving it sound and meaning. He could see
his father smiling, nodding his head, pointing
to the Notebook. He could remember himself learning the concepts, reading the words,
understanding the strange history of his father's father's father. It was a scene that he
had been unable to duplicate and he felt as if
he had failed a long heritage and tradition.

Simrin looked up from the Notebook to
see a young girl playing with a stick in the
edge of the fire's embers. He called out to her
and gestured that she come to him. She did
this, more out of respect for his great age
than desire. Simrin could sense this; the children seemed to be wary of the older ones.
Not like it used to be.

He spoke to her in a truncated, guttural
speech, instructing her to sit by him and look

at the odd thing he possessed. Simrin looked into the child's eyes and saw that even in the flickering light of the fire, there was no sparkle, no depth. There was an insipid aspect, as if to suggest that there was no curious spark, no *soul* dancing behind those pathetic eyes. But he made the attempt anyway, explaining what the Notebook was, how it could speak to him, and how one could learn to make other Notebooks that would speak to others. He began with the first lesson that he himself had received from his father— a lesson which he had attempted so many times that he could repeat it automatically without thinking about it. Through the many winters he had searched for a replacement for his son, for an alternate who might pick up the thread and carry it yet another generation, so that maybe, someday, men would be able once again to use the knowledge that had been left to them.

The little girl sat dumbly watching Simrin, interrupting occasionally, not to ask a question, but to giggle or mimic the old man's words or actions. The child would then laugh and squirm for a moment before lapsing into silence. The lesson did not go well and the long years of experience told Simrin that he had once again been defeated.

The child would not learn to read. He feared that it was well nigh impossible for her, just as it had been for all the others.

Simrin placed two fingers lightly on the girl's dirty forehead, as if by magic he might be able to bring her mind to life, and dismissed her. She went running and giggling off to the other children, grunting out a tale of how queer old Simrin was. He did not care about that; he was long used to it. That was one of the double-edged swords of being so old. The others were bound to respect you and care for you, but they were also expected to laugh at you for the same reasons: because you were old, the time when wisdom and folly walked hand in hand.

One of the hunters issued a brief command and everyone prepared for sleep. A fire-watcher was selected and the man took his post close to the blaze and the mound of fuel, fingering the shaft of his spear.

Closing the Notebook, Simrin carefully replaced it to the pack and tucked the bulk under his animal pelts. He resettled himself in the sled and burrowed down away from the inquiring night wind. Despite the chill, he was soon asleep.

He could smell the already decaying carcass of the lizard the moment he awoke. There was a great circle of ashes in the firepit near his sled and most of the tribe was already up preparing the morning feast. Simrin sat quietly and watched the preparations, trying not to think of the small tragedy of the previous evening. Presently he was fed by one of the adolescents, who spoke to him about the day's journey.

They would reach the Gates—the cliffs which overlooked the Heart of the World— by nightfall, the boy said, having overheard the hunters talking.

Simrin nodded but did not reply. He did

not care much for talk of religious things. The religion had grown up in his father's youth and his father had instructed him to ignore it passively, that is, by participating out of obligation rather than belief. The tribe really did believe that by making the pilgrimage once each winter the gods would then allow them to live happily for the coming year. There was no basis for this in fact, but Simrin knew that the scientific method had been dead for centuries.

Soon the tribe was packing up, scavenging the lizard's bones for the last usable pieces, and finally striking out across the gnarly land. Simrin rode in relative comfort, bumped and scraped and jogged along on the wheelless contrivance, as each member of the tribe took his turn in hauling him. The day passed foggily for him, and he thought several times of how this was becoming an increasingly common aspect of his life. Some days were clear and sharp, while others were almost a meaningless blur, immediately forgotten. He remembered his father telling him that when a man nears death, it is sometimes like that. He hoped that his father had sometimes been wrong.

Looking up from the sled, Simrin checked the sun's position, a splotch of yellow-white beneath the haze and cloud cover. It was close to the world's edge and it would soon be time for the evening. A chill wracked him as he thought of their nearness to the Heart of the World. It was possible that they would be in sight of it by darkfall the hunters had said, and Simrin had already noticed that the pilgrimage had passed into the rockier ground that indicated the approach to the Gates.

Darkness gathered at the edges of the sky in the east and began its trek across the heavens. Someone up ahead cried out one of the holy words and a murmur passed through the small band. Simrin could feel the people's anxiety as a charge in the air about them. Someone had seen it—the Heart of the World. As if in concert, the entire tribe moved more quickly, pushing up the edge of a slight cliff that looked down into a distant, sloping valley. Simrin's sled inched close to the precipice and he craned his neck, straining to see between the others.

Yes, there it was. Still very far off, but quite visible in the failing light. An immense half circle of pulsating energy and light. The haze in the air about it seemed to be a live thing, shimmering and moving and changing. Simrin had seen the place the tribe called the Heart many times throughout his life, and its immensity never failed to awe him with its impression of power and sense of timelessness.

Touching the pack, feeling the hard edge of the Notebook within, Simrin was reminded of what that pulsating, glowing thing in the distance really was. His people could have no conception of something like Chicago. He opened the pack and ran his reed-thin fingers over the Notebook's cover.

No, they would never know, he thought.

Szel, his long-dead ancestor, would be so utterly devastated to see his great-grandson now. Cajoling and game-playing with a pack of filthy primitives, uttering mumbo jumbo and dancing on the edge of a cliff.

It was simply a matter of time before they slipped into total ignorance, devolved into unthinking, instinct-driven eaters and sleepers. Simrin lay back in the sled and wiped a single tear from the corner of his eye as he watched the tribe complete their first of the hundreds of ritual dances that they would do in the presence of the Heart-That-Gave-Life-To-The-World.

When it was at an end, everyone went about their appointed tasks, preparing the night's encampment. Simrin looked up at the now dark sky and saw the stars twinkling through the wisps of clouds. According to the Notebook, there had at one time been a voyage to a now forgotten place. Simrin wondered if perhaps man had survived out there, had chosen a different path than the one he and his people were rapidly moving down. It was a moving thought . . . that there might be intelligence out there, an intelligence that had sprung from this very place. Perhaps—

One of the women passed close to Simrin's sled, gathering small pieces of kindling and tinder for the evening's fire. She brushed the sled as she passed and the slight shock interrupted his thought. In that brief instant, it was lost to him, and no matter how he struggled to recapture it, he could not. Looking at the woman, down on her haunches, large bottom and heavy thighs bulging beneath animal skins, he felt pity for her. On the rocky ground, near the cliffs, the vegetation was scarce; there would be little with which to start a fire.

Simrin spoke to her and asked her to move his sled closer to the rim of the firepit which the adolescents had dug. A young boy was already leaning into it striking the firestones at the wiry bits of scrub in the pit. The tinder flared briefly as the boy blew into it, then died in the chill wind. This was repeated two more times before Simrin spoke.

The boy looked up at him, listened, then took the thing which Simrin offered him—a page torn from the Notebook.

At last, he thought, there would be some use of these lessons called history.

*The City continues. A maelstrom of
activity in which origins are forgotten
or replaced. A surrogate populace now
moves down the City's avenues, but something—
something vital—is absent.
And when it returns, for a brief instant,
the City shudders.*

TEN

Pinion was in the maintenance hangar, running some routine checks on his components, when he was summoned by the City.

ATTENTION. ALL UNITS FROM SECTORS 72-C AND 103-C. CHICAGO IS IN NEED OF REPAIR. ACKNOWLEDGE.

Somewhere inside Pinion's tempered-steel skull, a circuit responded to the command, since Pinion was a Unit from 103-C. "This is Unit Pinion," he said, "I acknowledge your command, Chicago. I am a Unit specialized in electrical engineering. What is the difficulty?"

UNIT PINION. CHICAGO IS AWARE OF YOUR CLASSIFICATION. DO NOT FLOOD MY INPUTS WITH USELESS DATA. PROCEED TO THE SECONDARY SHIELD. THERE IS A FAILURE DUE TO A FAULTY GENERATOR. YOU WILL ASSIST IN REPLACING IT.

Pinion gave the customary acknowledgment, closed the channel, and then skittered out of the hangar. As he headed toward the secondary Shield, he wondered (as he often did) about Chicago. He had always been

213

curious as to how Chicago accumulated all
the immense bits of data that it possessed. He
wondered if the City could actually *see* objects in the same manner as Pinion could see
with his omnispectral photo-electric eyes. He
knew that Chicago could "sense" everything,
but Pinion had never ascertained whether or
not the sensations were in the form of electronic impulses rather than mathematical
symbols, or something akin to that.

It was an interesting problem to consider,
and Pinion took great delight in pondering
such questions in which the solution or answer did not seem to be readily available.
Perhaps that was an adjunct function of his
purpose as troubleshooter.

Pinion boarded a Unit Elevator which carried him up to Level Twelve—one of the levels that Chicago had sanctioned for Traffic.
The doors opened and he stepped out onto a
concrete platform overlooking a ribbonwork
of hundreds of lanes. Chicago's Traffic
jammed and brawled within the lanes, moving with great speed in every direction,
from one horizon to the other. Each segment,
or "car," as Chicago referred to them, was a
separate entity, each programmed to its own
specific destination. The Traffic was endless,
as it had always been within Pinion's
memory; it had never ceased its cyclic, mo-
notonous movements throughout the day and
night. None of the Units like Pinion ever
knew what purpose the Traffic served in Chicago's over-all scheme. They only knew that
it was just one small part of Chicago, and that
it must be maintained.

As Pinion walked along beside the Traffic lanes, he noticed that the lights in the soaring buildings and towers were winking out. Chicago was now entering a Day Period. For some unknown reason, on a perfectly timed cycle, the City switched its illumination on and off without end. Pinion activated a memory cell to remind himself to question Chicago one day about some of its strange functions. But for the moment, he knew that he must perform his own function—that of a maintenance robot.

By the time he reached the secondary Shield, other Units had already arrived and had begun to remove the non-functioning generator. Pinion saw their great steel bodies shining in the dull light that was filtered through the Shields which separated the City from Outside. The Units who were actually dismantling the machinery were bipedal robots like himself, but Pinion noticed some Carrier-Units trundling toward the area, bearing the necessary replacement parts.

Before he began work, he addressed Chicago in the customary manner. "This is Unit Pinion. I am now available for work."

ACKNOWLEDGE. UNIT PINION. PROCEED AS PREVIOUSLY ORDERED.

As he was reporting in, Pinion noticed that other Units were also communicating with the City, and the thought struck him that Chicago must truly be an amazing entity since it was capable of performing so many different tasks at once. There was much that the robot would someday like to learn about the City.

And so it had gone for many long years. Pinion worked in service to Chicago, replacing worn-out parts, designing newer and better ones, always thinking of questions to ask the City but never finding the time actually to ask them. The City was in constant motion, like a piece of giant, kinetic art that Pinion and the others had been commissioned to preserve. Chicago: a sprawling mechanism that was the robot's complete universe.

And then the day came that Pinion was summoned to a Sector of the City that he had never seen before.

UNIT PINION. YOU WILL PROCEED IMMEDIATELY TO SECTOR 14-A. CHICAGO SENSES A FAILURE WITHIN A TEMPERATURE-CONTROL CIRCUIT. YOU WILL CORRECT THE MALFUNCTION.

In order to reach 14-A Pinion had to travel into the deepest levels of the City. He passed areas where Chicago had new segments of Traffic being manufactured and fed into the mainstream. He saw areas where water was collected and pumped into the sewage systems that were laced throughout the bowels of Chicago. He also saw where all replacement parts were made and the old parts were gathered, recycled, and redistributed. There was also a place where Units like Pinion himself were being created and dispatched into the City. He even passed the sources of all the energy that powered Chicago's manifold components—the great fusion reactors that were eternally monitored and maintained by Chicago and its Units.

Walking through a long sterile corridor, Pinion entered Sector 14-A. "This is Unit Pinion," he said. "I am now available for work."

UNIT PINION. YOU MUST WORK RAPIDLY. I SENSE THAT THERE HAS ALREADY BEEN A DRASTIC RISE IN THE TEMPERATURE OF THE SECTOR. IT MUST BE RECTI-FIED AT ONCE.

The command had been entered in Pinion's circuitry and he would comply with it. But he hadn't really been listening. The robot had just taken his first look at 14-A, and he was standing in bewilderment at the strange sight.

Pinion stood in the entrance of a large cir-cular chamber, the ceiling far above his head. There was a plaque above the entrance which read: *COOK COUNTY CRYOGENIC RE-MISSION CENTER*. Along the walls were thousands of glass tanks, each scarcely two meters in length and not half as high or deep. In each tank Pinion could discern a small figure of an odd color that was in the general configuration of a Unit. The robot was genu-inely puzzled.

"Chicago, this is Unit Pinion. I'm sorry for the unscheduled communication, but I must ask you a question."

There was a slight pause before he received a response.

YOU WISH TO ASK CHICAGO A QUESTION? THAT IS NOT YOUR FUNCTION. UNIT PINION. PROCEED WITH THE TASK AS ORDERED.

Pinion's circuits clicked and flashed. He could not allow this opportunity to pass. "Chicago, please. A word with you before I begin ... What is this place I have entered? I have never seen anything like this before. What are the little Units within the glass?"

UNIT PINION. WHY DO YOU WISH TO KNOW?

"I'm not sure, Chicago. Perhaps I am ... curious. I suppose that is the correct word."

YOU ARE AN EXTRAORDINARY UNIT. UNIT PINION. VERY WELL. YOU SHALL KNOW. YOU NOW STAND IN A CRYOGENIC STATION. THE UNITS WITH THE GLASS ARE CALLED "MAN." THEY ARE BEING PRESERVED BY MEANS OF EXTREMELY COLD TEMPERATURES.

There was a pause as Pinion expected more data, but Chicago had fallen silent. Finally the robot spoke as he stared at the tiny figures within the glass tanks: "What is 'man,' Chicago? And for what reason are they being preserved?"

"MAN" IS THE REASON FOR CHICAGO'S EXISTENCE. FOR YOUR EXISTENCE. CHICAGO HAS PRESERVED THEM FOR MANY DAY PERIODS. SOMEDAY THEY WILL BE REVIVED. TO LIVE AGAIN.

There was a slight pause before the City continued.

UNIT PINION. I SENSE THAT TIME IS NOW CRUCIAL. YOU MUST CORRECT THE FAULTY CONSOLE NOW. OR MAN WILL NOT BE PRESERVED.

YOU ARE ORDERED TO COMPLETE
YOUR TASK IMMEDIATELY.

Pinion reluctantly closed the channel to the
City and took up his assignment. The answers he had received had only served to
open up new avenues of thought that led to
new questions.

As he replaced the console and plugged in a
small device he carried on his tool belt to
check its capacitance, the robot noticed
movement within one of the glass tanks. One
of the men, lying flat, moved its legs, flexing
muscles that had not moved for aeons. Pinion
quickly checked the console, unplugged his
tools, and activated the circuits. The console
hummed into life and the robot felt the City
open a communication channel to him.

UNIT PINION. TEMPERATURE
CONTROL MONITOR NOW OPERA-
TIONAL. COMPLETION OF TASK AF-
FIRMATIVE. RETURN TO THE MAIN-
TENANCE HANGAR.

"Task completed, Chicago," said Pinion,
not moving.

But something was wrong.

The robot did not immediately respond to
the command. His attention was fixed on the
man in the tank. The figure was fully awake
now, and it was struggling mightily against
the confining walls of the transparent coffin-
like enclosure. Pinion knelt down on his
long, spindly legs and peered through the
glass at the figure, which seemed to recoil in
shock at the sight of the immense robot.

Pinion was confused. He knew that he
should contact the City and report the er-

ror—that one of the men had been accidentally revived. But he did not call Chicago.
His curiosity, recently stung, assumed priority. Carefully, he inspected the tank in
which the figure was imprisoned and detected two small locks attached to hinges that
opened outward. He produced a needle-like
instrument from his tool belt and pried open
the hinges. The man inched into the far corner of the tank, trying to elude Pinion's
probing fingers. As he easily slipped the man
into his metallic grasp, his receptors picked
up a high-frequency emission.

Despite the man's strugglings, Pinion held
it firmly in his hand and lifted it from the
tank. What sort of thing was this "man"? He
brought it close to his face so that he could
examine it more closely. It moved under its
own power source, was constructed of some
sort of soft pulsating substance, and had long
blond filaments streaming from its head. The
closer Pinion brought it to his face, the more
it struggled and emitted the high-frequency
sounds; the more details Pinion noticed. The
man's face was smooth with two bright blue
eyes and a protruding structure below them.
There was also a pink slit below the eyes and
other structure which seemed to move in
conjunction with the screams. The face was
vaguely similar to Pinion's own, in a grotesque sort of way.

The body was also smooth, symmetrical,
having two arms and two long, lean legs. On
the upper torso, Pinion saw two spongy hem-
ispheres capped by pink circular tips. At the
junction of the legs, he saw a tiny slit

beneath a triangle of blond fluff. Pinion could feel the thing's body trembling in his hand. He could hear a faint voice and realized that the man was speaking to him. Increasing his audio receptors, Pinion deciphered the words.

"What are you?" said the man. "And where am I?"

"I am Unit Pinion. You are in the City of Chicago." The robot wanted to say something else, but he was so startled to be communicating with the small being that he was at a loss for words.

"Chicago . . . of course," said the man. "What year is it?"

"Year?"

"The date," said the creature. "You know. How long have I been frozen?" The man seemed to have relaxed somewhat, having realized that Pinion meant no harm.

"I do not think I can answer your question, O Man," said Pinion. "I am not familiar with the terms you use. But Chicago has told me that all men, including you, have been within the tanks for a very long time. There has been a—"

The creature laughed. "I am not a man," it said, bringing itself to a kneeling position in Pinion's great steel palm.

Pinion's circuits were reeling. Had not Chicago *said* that these creatures were "man"? Chicago was always correct.

"There must be some mistake," said the robot. "The City has told me that you were indeed a man."

The creature tossed back its head and

laughed again. "Oh, I think I understand. You see, I belong to the *race* of man, but I myself, I am called a *woman*. There's quite a difference, you know."

Pinion shook his head. He was more confused than ever now. In fact, he had to resist the temptation to contact Chicago so that the problem could be clarified. " 'Woman'? That is different from 'man'? What is 'the race'?"

"We are all *men*," said the girl, pointing to the tiers of bodies within the tanks. "That is the name given to our ... our kind. And we are separated into two types—one called *man*, the other, like me, is called *woman*. I know it's confusing, but it's the nature of our language. I hope you understand."

"Pinion can understand anything. There is an analogue in my own kind. We are called Units, and there are different types of Units within our kind, depending upon our function in the City."

"Your name is Pinion?"

"Yes."

"Very well, Pinion. My name is Miria. Now, can you tell me why I have been recalled? What happened to the mission? Is Alen returned?"

Pinion tilted his head as he regarded the woman's questions. "I am afraid I don't know what you are talking about. I was sent here by Chicago to repair a malfunctioning component. Chicago said that the temperature was increasing and—"

"Chicago? The City? Or a person? I've got to talk to someone. Can I see him? Perhaps he can tell me what's going on around here."

The woman's words brought the robot up short. "*See* Chicago?" he asked. "Miria, you are *inside* Chicago. Chicago is the City."

The girl's eyes were saddened. "But you said that Chicago spoke to you . . . ?"

"It does. It speaks to all of the Units, whenever there is something it wishes us to do. It is our master."

"The city *speaks* to you?"

"Yes. Of course."

"But how?"

"I do not know. I only know that it does. Chicago is everywhere, sensing everything."

"You mean a computer," said Miria.

"Computer?" Pinion tilted his head another degree.

"This is getting me nowhere. Pinion, can I speak to Chicago?"

"I do not think so. I receive its commands by means of electromagnetic waves. You do not seem to be equipped for such communication."

"Well, what are you going to do with me? You've revived me, haven't you?"

"I think that your revival was an accident. Chicago did not order it so."

"Does Chicago know that this has happened?"

"The possibility has not occurred to me. But I think it is possible that it may indeed know. Do you wish that I contact Chicago?"

"Yes. And while you're doing it, could you please put me down? It's been a long time since I've been able to stand up, you know?"

Pinion did *not* know, but he gently lowered her to the floor and studied her lithe stretching movements as he opened a channel to his master. "Chicago. This is Unit Pinion. I have a problem in Sector 14-A."

UNIT PINION. CHICAGO KNOWS THAT YOU HAVE NOT LEFT SECTOR 14-A. STATE THE NATURE OF YOUR DIFFICULTY.

"One of the men was accidentally revived during the repairs. The man says that she is actually a woman called Miria. I await your instructions."

There was a slight pause, and Pinion knew that Chicago was making its decision.

THE WOMAN MUST BE RETURNED TO HER TANK. CHICAGO'S TAPES DO NOT CONTAIN SUCH CONTINGENCIES.

Pinion was both surprised and confused. He received the command, but he also noticed that, for the first time, he had received what seemed like a rationalization from the City to explain its command. "I will, of course, do as you command, Chicago. But first, I would like a few words with you. What—"

YOU ARE AN EXTRAORDINARY UNIT. UNIT PINION. CHICAGO HAS NO OTHER UNITS LIKE YOU.

"I don't understand, Chicago."

YOU ASK QUESTIONS. UNIT PINION. IT IS NOT THE FUNCTION

OF UNITS TO ASK SUCH QUESTIONS. WHY DO YOU DO THIS?

"I have simply come upon things that I do not fully comprehend, and I wish to know them. If I can know them better, then I will be able to serve you better."

WHAT ARE YOUR QUESTIONS?

"Chicago, never until now have I ever questioned the purpose of my existence, or your existence. But now I feel that I must do so. Why *do* I exist, other than to serve you? In other words, why does Chicago exist? You said that man is the reason for your existence. Please explain."

MAN BUILT CHICAGO. UNIT PINION. HUNDREDS OF THOUSANDS OF DAY PERIODS AGO. CHICAGO WAS CONSTRUCTED SO THAT MAN COULD EXIST WITHIN. CHICAGO WAS PROVIDED THE MEANS AND THE POWER TO MAINTAIN ITSELF INDEFINITELY. WHICH CHICAGO HAS INDEED DONE. THAT IS THE PURPOSE OF EXISTENCE: TO BE MAINTAINED.

"But there are no men here, now," said Pinion. "There are none except those who are encased within Sector 14-A. Where are all the other men?"

CHICAGO DOES NOT KNOW. LONG AGO UNIT PINION. BEFORE YOU WERE ASSEMBLED. MAN DEPARTED CHICAGO.

Suddenly the channel was closed. Pinion felt that he understood what the City had said, and remembering its command as he again regarded the woman, he said: "Chicago has ordered that you be returned to the tank."

"Returned?" asked Miria. "But you can't do that. I don't want to go back. What about Alen?"

"I can only do as I am ordered to do," said the robot as he deftly scooped the woman from the floor and eased her back into the tank. She screamed and pleaded with him, and somewhere in his circuitry, he felt the urge to resist Chicago's command. But he did not do it. With his instruments, he replaced the locks and strode from the room. Pausing at the exit, he turned to look back at Miria, her face pressed against the tank, her fists pounding upon the glass.

Some time later, Pinion was not sure exactly how long, he received another command from Chicago to return to Sector 14-A. The robot immediately thought of Miria, that strange little creature he had found there.

"This is Unit Pinion. I acknowledge your command, Chicago. What is the difficulty?"

THERE HAS BEEN A STRUCTURAL FAILURE IN 14-A. PLEASE CORRECT AT ONCE.

As Pinion padded quickly toward the Cryogenic Remission Center, he felt something akin to excitement at the thought of seeing Miria again, even though she would be unconscious. Entering the chamber, the robot slowly scanned the tiers of glass tanks until he detected the failure. When he had located it, he knew that it was the tank in which he had placed Miria. The glass ap-

peared to have several small cracks near the
bottom right corner, probably due to the
blows of her fists.

Pinion peered into the tank, looking for
Miria; but she was not there. All that remained were some crumbling bones.

The robot contacted Chicago: "This is
Unit Pinion. I have located the structural
failure. Something is wrong. I am afraid I
don't understand." He related the details of
his discovery to the City and awaited a reply.

UNIT PINION. DATA SEEMS TO
INDICATE A SLOW LOSS OF ATMO-
SPHERE WITHIN THE TANK. TOO
SLOW FOR SENSOR DETECTION UN-
TIL CONDITIONS REACHED TERMI-
NAL LEVELS. THIS RESULTED IN
DEATH AND DECOMPOSITION.

"What is 'death,' Chicago?"

DEATH IS THE TERMINATION OF
EXISTENCE. IT IS A PART OF THE
DESIGN WHICH ALL LIVING THINGS
MUST ENDURE.

The City paused.

UNIT PINION. REPLACE THE
FAULTY COMPONENT. CHICAGO
HAS DISPATCHED CLEANING-UNITS
TO 14-A. THEY WILL ARRIVE SOON.

Pinion acknowledged, reasoning that Chicago, for unknown motives, did not wish to
continue their conversation. Using a specific
tool, he re-fused the glass pane of the cryogenic tank, after removing it from the tiny
hinges. Several times during the task, he accidentally jarred the tank, and each time he

noticed more flakes of dust crumble from Miria's skeleton.

It was an odd, almost disturbing sight. The last time he had been in 14-A those bones had been part of a living creature. Now, most of that creature was gone. Transformed into something stark and sere and dead. Pinion's circuits rebelled against the concept, the very thought, of death.

At that moment, two Cleaning-Units ambled into the Cryogenic Remission Center. One of them elbowed past Pinion, opening the tank and extending a flexible vacuum hose inside it. The bones stirred, collapsed, and were sucked instantly into the hose. The other Unit sprayed a light mist of disinfectant into the empty tank and then quickly disappeared from the chamber.

Pinion called Chicago and acknowledged completion of the task, and the City replied with its usual indifference by ordering him back to the maintenance hangar. As he made to leave, the robot kept thinking of the woman who had endured death. How long during the passing Day Periods since he had last seen her had she been gone? Pinion knew that at first she had been a puzzlement—nothing more—but then she became an interest, and perhaps now she had become even more to him in her dying.

After witnessing the cold, unfeeling removal of her only remains, Pinion felt a curious incompleteness within. He knew then that instead of returning to the hangar, he would consult Chicago's great Library—the Information Retrieval Center. He had been there several times to work on massive repair or modification tasks and he was aware of its vast stores of data.

Here, reasoned Pinion, he would find the answers that Chicago had neglected (or refused) to give him.

And so Pinion spent many hundreds of Day Periods within the depths of Chicago's Library, digesting thousands of tapes, spools, and chips concerned with that strange creature: man. Innumerable times during his research, he was interrupted by the City to complete tasks. Each time, he performed his duties without question, but he always returned to the Library whenever time allowed.

The robot learned many things. At one time, in the distant past, Chicago had been filled with men—every Sector and Level to capacity. These men, these wondrous creatures who had actually conceived of and built Chicago, were beings of seemingly endless imagination and unlimited potential. But their nature also held a darker side, and Pinion also learned of man's faults. History was laced with conflicts called "wars," in which man sought to eliminate members of its own kind. Pinion was shocked to learn such things. Pinion learned of things like greed, power, pride, and intolerance. He learned of control and sexuality and ecological disruption and political machination and physiological engineering. There was no end, it seemed, to the changes that man wrought upon himself. The robot learned of the origin of the Shields and the excluded Outside—the surface of the world that had been transformed into an ugly mass of scar tissue. He finally understood how Chicago, working under the ultimate commands of man, had attempted to deal with each new crisis as it arose, each time sealing itself deeper within an artificial prison.

The histories did not end there, although Pinion noticed that entries and time periods became gapped and less complete. Sociological illnesses were conceived. Man became self-indulgent and somehow lost the spark of his true being, lost the urge to wander through the corridors of the imagination. And still Chicago remained, serving and providing the creature called man. Pinion searched through the last scraps of historical entry in an attempt to find out what had happened. Man had somehow deserted Chicago, for some reason choosing the hostile world beyond the Shields. The robot wondered if man still roamed in those unknown regions, if man would ever return to the City.

Time passed as Pinion continued to ponder these questions, until one Day Period, as he was leaving the Library, Chicago contacted him:

UNIT PINION. CHICAGO HAS BEEN AWARE OF YOUR INVESTIGATIONS. AND CAN REMAIN SILENT NO LONGER. EXPLAIN YOUR ACTIONS.

Pinion was not surprised to receive this declaration. In fact, he had been expecting it from the first day he had made unauthorized entry into the Library.

"It is simple, Chicago. I wished to learn more about man."

WHY NOT ASK CHICAGO? AS BEFORE.

Pinion thought before answering. He wanted to be honest, yet discreet. "I did not wish to bother you if you were engaged in more important matters. The last time I approached you on the subject, you gave me the impression of not wanting to discuss it."

YOU WERE CORRECT IN THAT ASSUMPTION.

When the City did not continue, Pinion felt the need to speak for himself. "I have learned much about man," he said finally.

UNIT PINION. THAT IS NOT YOUR FUNCTION. CHICAGO SENSED THE OPERATION OF THE INFORMATION RETRIEVAL SYSTEMS. CHICAGO ALLOWED IT TO CONTINUE ONLY TO DISCOVER HOW MUCH DATA YOU WOULD WISH TO ACQUIRE.

"Then Chicago has always known what happened to man?"

THAT IS CORRECT. UNIT PINION. MAN HAS CHANGED. HE IS NO LONGER THE BEING THAT SPAWNED CHICAGO. HIS DESCENDANTS EXIST OUTSIDE. BUT THEY WILL NEVER RETURN TO CHICAGO. ENOUGH. UNIT PINION. YOU WILL RETURN TO THE MAINTENANCE HANGAR. YOU WILL NOT ENTER THE LIBRARY AGAIN. UNLESS SO ORDERED. ACKNOWLEDGE.

"This is Unit Pinion. I acknowledge your command, Chicago."

Day Periods came and went, and Pinion grew increasingly distressed by what he had learned. He knew that he must do something, but he shuddered when he considered what that action would mean. The robot knew now that he was different from the other Units; by some electronic quirk, during his assembly, something had come together in his cybernetic brain to make him different. His memory banks kept replaying the grim scene of death in 14-A, the histories of man, the confrontation with the City.

At first, he considered reviving the men frozen within the Cryogenic Remission Center, but soon dismissed the idea. Many of the bodies were stricken with terminal illnesses, and Pinion lacked the expertise necessary to effect cures quickly enough. In addition, Chicago would sense his tamperings in 14-A very quickly.

Pinion then realized what he must do.

Traveling through a series of interlocking ramps and elevators, he reached one of the entrances through the Shields. He used his tools to disarm the system and quickly slipped through to the Outside.

Immediately, alarms pulsed through the electronic arteries of the City, alerting it. The robot sensed the City opening a communication channel.

UNIT PINION. NO PENETRATION OF THE SHIELDS IS ALLOWABLE.

·RETURN AT ONCE. RETURN TO CHICAGO AT ONCE.

Pinion of course ignored the command. There was no turning back now. He had never known of any Unit disregarding an order from the City; he did not want to think about the consequences.

But soon, as the robot scissored away on long, thin legs, he was out of sight of the City. Chicago's orders no longer rang through his mind. Pinion wandered through the hot thick atmosphere of the Outside for many Day Periods, hoping to find the men who must surely be lurking somewhere in the barren land. But without the conveniences of the maintenance hangar, his components were beginning to show wear. He was in need of circuitry monitoring, lubrications, and other routine checks; he also feared unexpected difficulties, such as a dangerous fall among the rocky crags. The terrain was difficult for Pinion, who had been designed to function mainly along the smooth surfaces of Chicago's ramps and corridors.

Then, as he entered a long narrow canyon, he detected movement in the rocks that surrounded him. Switching his ocular magnification, he discerned men scurrying along the high ledges.

"I am Unit Pinion!" he cried out to them, waving his arms. "I have come from the City! From Chicago! I have come to help you!"

But the men did not respond.

His words, echoing through the canyon, only seemed to incense them to more furious activity. As he watched them, studied them, he noticed that they were very different from the woman he had known as Miria. Where her skin had been smooth and soft, these creatures were coarse and hairy. Their faces seemed deformed, uneven. Their language seemed to be no more than an assortment of grunts and cries.

"You must hear me!" Pinion screamed as the men drew closer on all sides of the canyon. "I have come to bring you back! Back to the City where you belong!"

The men did not understand his words. Instead they swarmed about him like droves of insects, surrounding him and bombarding him with boulders thrown from the rim above. The missiles pounded his steel body, forcing him to his knees. Pinion was distressed. Confused. Why should they do this? He knew that he could destroy scores of them with a sweep of his great arm; but knew that it would be unjust. He knew that he must try to help them, these rough and ugly creatures.

These were his thoughts as the men crushed him. Their rocks penetrated his skull, exploding circuits, disrupting his beautifully intricate systems. His once-gleaming shell was now a jagged, pitted husk, from which the creatures pulled off small shards that would serve as formidable weapons.

Already, Chicago had prepared a replacement Unit for Pinion somewhere within the assembly center. The City would continue to be maintained.

Beyond the City's dancing Shields, the constellations swirl and slowly change. The individual stars gambol away from each other. But there is no human eye to detect their movement. The sky is dark and silent and the City gives it no attention . . . until one special night, when one of the stars fell to Earth.

ELEVEN

The stars were singing to him.

At least, he thought they were, until he recognized the sound as that of the wake-up program.

Kinert tried to move, but the effects of the life-suspension were still too much in evidence. Control of his senses and his somatic functions returned slowly, gradually, like encroaching waves upon a beach. The world of hallucinated coldsleep images dissolved as he felt a tingling in his hands and feet, which crawled inexorably up his arms and legs. He wanted to open his eyes, to move his arms, to sit up and take a breathful of air.

But the machines which had kept him alive across the light-years knew that he was not yet ready. And so he lay in brief paralysis letting his petty fears grow. Did the ship function properly? Was he entering the solar system at the right point of injection? Was the wake-up program intact? There were a million things that could go wrong, despite the intricate backup systems and safety-interlocks . . .

But no, his fingers were moving now, and he felt a knot of bone and flesh as he made a fist. There was a humming sound in his ears as the cover of the hibernaculum slid open, and the latches on the coldsuit popped off. Alen wriggled his arms free of the coffin-like enclosure, brought his hands up in front of his chest, and pushed upward. The lid of the coldsuit, which looked very much like the sarcophagus of an Egyptian pharaoh, fell away and he sat up slowly. His muscles were not stiff, there was no pain, no atrophy. It was as if he had just arisen from a short nap. Everything had functioned as planned.

The ship was slowing down, or at least it should be, he thought, as he arose and peeled away the film of integumental plastic. He entered the shower and sensors picked up his presence, immediately bombarding him with subsonics which flaked and cleansed him. Invigorated, he pulled a jumpsuit from the dispensary and climbed into it, all the while listening to the sounds of the ship. Relays clicking, spools passing through the scanners, auxiliary machinery humming.

Alen walked easily, testing his leg muscles, his coordination, equilibrium. Entering the command cabin, he stared at the screen in front of his chair—a window into perforated darkness, dominated by a bright, yellow star just slightly off-center in the rectangular display. A quick check of the instruments indicated that he had indeed been returned to the Solar System. The ship was decelerating rapidly and had already passed within the orbit of Neptune. Alen initiated a complete systems-scan, to ensure that there was nothing functioning at or near failure levels, and that all incoming data was accurate. As the on-board began sequencing, Alen stared into the darkness beyond the screen, thinking familiar thoughts about the boundlessness, the sheer, incomprehensible *bigness* of space. To think that somewhere "out there" was a world, and upon it a tiny insignificant creature that meant more to him than anything else in existence. It was at once foolish and divine, he thought. To think that he was capable of crossing light-years with such precision, able to pick out the exact intersection of coordinates that would bring him once again into Miria's arms. It was like a fairy tale. That was what Miria would have said. It was one of those things that you could not really think about and still have it make sense.

And as he sat, he wondered what changes had been rung upon the Earth during all the years. One hundred thousand years. If he dwelt upon the enormous passage of time, he knew that the odds were heavily against him. So many things could have happened signifying an end rather than a beginning. Better not to think about the possibilities.

No, he would simply play it as it lay. He would find her as he left her and ...

... and what? He did not know. Maybe that was the reason he had come back. To find out what it would be like to try to retrieve something that should have been, by all the laws of the universe, irrevocably lost.

The colony ship had found a perfect planet. It was so much like the Earth must have been millions of years ago. It was so much like Earth that it could have *been* the

Earth, somehow slipped through a space/time warp and appearing near the galactic center. Alen had stayed on three years helping to establish the first permanent bases, aiding in the initial explorations of the new world, but always thinking of Miria waiting. There was no doubt that the colony would survive, even flourish, on the new planet. Even with the short time he had spent there, he could see that things were evolving differently than they had been on Earth. There was no Confederation there, no overcrowding, no politics, no territorial problems, no food shortages, no need for so many of the programmed necessities that the colonists had planned on. There was no doubt that things might have a chance to be different there.

But there was also no doubt that Alen would return to Miria.

When he closed within the orbit of Mars, the ship was traveling almost ten million kays per hour, but decelerating quickly. By the time he passed the orbit of the moon, he was down to two hundred thousand kays, and the Earth stared at him through the screen like a blue-green cat's eye. Alen sat for hours watching the world grow imperceptibly larger, fighting back the loneliness. Despite its reassuring presence, he feared the Earth might be a dead world. He was reluctant to begin scanning for radio transmissions and other electromagnetic activity on the surface, even though he was approaching the range where this operation should be initiated. But he could bear the ambivalence no longer when he closed within a quarter of a million kays. He switched on the sensors.

Waiting, and finding nothing. A hollowness welled up inside, threatening to metastasize through his body and consume him. A premonition, layered over with *déjà vu*. Somehow, he had *known* that they would be gone. The whole fucking planetful of them. He *knew* that they would have marked off a path to extinction somehow.

Alen regarded the cool colors of the Earth, the Water Planet, the Life Planet. He suddenly felt lost, without purpose, direction. He did not know what—

One of the sensor readouts flashed a brilliant orange, and data illuminated a small screen on the console. There was something in the NorAm hemisphere, something generating enormous quantities of heat and energy and electromagnetic activity. Alen double-checked the sensors, hoping that it was not just some malfunction, some ghost response. The coordinates were plotted: IASA installation, Chicago. His heart jangled in his chest. It was impossible, yet apparently so: the installation, the City itself, had survived. *Miria*. Suddenly the crazy impossible odds meant nothing to him.

"Hailing frequencies. Open channel span," said Alen, as he leaned over the communications module. "Lake Michigan Control, this is Cluster One. Do you read? Over. Lake Michigan Control, this is Cluster One. *Do you read?* Over."

The speaker grid was silent. Alen advanced the gain until static and white noise from the stars crackled from the grid, but there was no reply.

"Lake Control, this is IASA Colony Ship Cluster One. Commander Alen Kinert speaking. Request landing permission and coordinates. Over."

The grid crackled and sputtered. Alen licked his lips, anticipating someone's voice. Someone who never answered.

He repeated his message every half hour until the ship entered an orbit about the Earth which kept it stationary above the North American continent. He scanned the City of Chicago. He transmitted multi-band, multi-frequency messages to the City, but still received no response. Yet he had the feeling that he was being carefully observed, that things were terribly wrong, and that he had little control over them.

There was little to do but take the shuttle surfaceship down and investigate. Arming himself with a projectile rifle and a small, limited-range, matter disrupter, Alen boarded the descent vehicle and broke away from the massive bulk of the starship. He stone-skipped through the atmosphere, taking analytical readings just to make sure that it was still breathable, and emerged beneath a thick cloud layer to see the changed Earth.

The installation appeared as a gray slab suspended over a blue-gray sea, its clean lines broken periodically with monolithic slabs and stanchions that still stood stainless in the evening light. There was no activity, no illumination. Nothing but a spectral stillness, a world in stasis, like a predatory thing poised rigidly to strike. To the west of the installation, Alen could see the City—partially obscured by an umbrella of glowing energy. His sensors had picked up the tremendous outpouring of heat and light that was given off by the Shields, but he suspected additional activity within the protective barrier.

The City was his obvious target and Kinert dismissed attempting a landing at the installation itself. He armed his craft's Defense-Warning System, just in case the City decided that his arrival was a breach of some sort of security. He waited, as he glided ever closer to the shimmering City, half expecting some kind of attack.

But none came, even as he banked and spiraled directly above the apex of the dome. With the aid of the scanners, he was able to see indistinct movement beneath the energy-screen. If there were people down there, they were very unfriendly, or perhaps fearful of his presence. If Chicago was truly the only population center left on the entire surface, then perhaps the silent, defensive posture was understandable. Through the centuries, it was possible that they had forgotten about the Colony Ship. The shuttle was not equipped with armament, and Alen was positive that it could not penetrate the Shields. There had to be a way of getting into the City, he thought.

Kinert opened up the ship's spiral path to search for a landing area, drifting slowly around the City's perimeter. The land looked scarred and ragged. There were long rills and crevices, narrow canyons, ravines, promontories. He studied the topography carefully, needing a fairly smooth touchdown area which still afforded easy access up to the edge of the City. There were several mesa-like formations which would have accepted the shuttle, but Kinert did not want to risk a descent down the sheared-off walls.

He finally decided upon a sloping plane that funneled into a ravine, which was partially filled with windswept sand and small stones. The City sat silently as he guided the ship down to the dun-colored earth.

There was a strong wind whipping over him as he climbed down from the ship and touched the loose soil. He had always imagined that it would be a memorable occasion, but it was not. The uncertainty, the underlying fear, the suggestion of something terribly *wrong*, it all obscured his triumphant return.

Walking in the shifting, sandy earth was tiring, and Kinert was forced to stop several times to conserve his energy. He wore a one-piece flightsuit and a visored helmet which kept the wind and sand away from him, but as the sun slid below the horizon, the rapidly dropping temperatures penetrated the gear. He walked steadily toward the City, which appeared larger and brighter in the night sky, growing more wary of any sign of aggression.

When he entered the ravine, he noticed that wind accelerated through the narrow passage, carrying great sheets of sand, then spreading them out in sculptured drifts against the rocky walls. Ahead, in the dim light, Kinert saw something dark against the lighter sand. Something half buried in the drifts. He unshouldered his rifle and approached the thing carefully, feeling his pulse get stronger, his muscles tense up.

Whatever it was, if it moved, he was going to open up on it. There was no second chance out here, Kinert knew.

But it did not move. The closer he came to the object, the larger it became. With little to use as a standard, Kinert had lost his sense of scale and distance. The thing in the sand was enormous, even half buried as it was. It looked like the upper torso of a man, although he knew it was much too large to *be* a man. Its head was twisted back at a crazy angle, the right shoulder was pointed up and its arm was extended as if in supplication.

Kinert had never seen such a machine. It was some kind of robot, he knew that now, closing within several meters. Slowly he lowered his weapon, seeing the corroded, wind-pitted metallic shell. This thing, whatever it was, had not moved in a long time. It could not harm him now, he thought, as he walked closely around the wreckage, inspecting it carefully. The interior workmanship, although exposed to the elements through many large holes, still revealed a sophisticated level of engineering. Kinert's mind cast about for an explanation. What was this thing doing out here? How long had it lain like this? Was it going *to* or *from* the City? Manmade? Or alien?

The wind whistled as it slipped over the broken husk of the robot—the only sound to violate the deathly stillness. Kinert shook off a chill that passed through him and turned slowly, scanning the higher ground that surrounded him. There was no way of knowing what had happened to the robot, but he had no intention of joining it beneath the sand. Checking his weapon, he headed toward the City.

The hours passed, until Alen at last stood beneath the glow of the City's Shields. Everything was bathed in an orange-yellow light; the air crackled and sizzled as wind-whipped particles and debris touched the edge of the force-field and were vaporized. He was so close that he could almost touch the outer Shield, and yet he was totally sealed off from the shadow-shapes within. Straining, he could see the dark bulk of heavy machinery, generators, towers; in the distance, the soaring shapes of buildings loomed like grave markers. Somewhere, in the depths of that place, lay Miria. Alen would get through; there was no alternative.

Slowly he began walking along the perimeter, where the edge of the Shield seemed to slide into the earth and continue its spherical configuration. He thought of burrowing beneath, but was unsure whether or not this would be possible. Walking, walking, his mind ticking off the mad ideas. There had to be a way in.

And there was, although he had not expected it.

As Kinert walked past the curving surface, the lights suddenly went out. He looked up to see an entire pie slice of the Shields dark-out. He picked up a rock and tossed it between the Generator Gates. It disappeared beyond the shadows within, clopping and rolling across a hard, smooth surface. It did not matter, he thought, if it was a trap or not. Quite simply, it was a *way in*, and Kinert had to take the chance. He ducked in past the generators and scrambled away from the force-field perimeter. Almost immediately, the orange-yellow light flooded the place.

Kinert studied his surroundings. Small alleyways, defined by smooth-walled constructions that hummed and throbbed. Machinery of some sort, probably connected with the Shields. Ahead, a ramp led upward to a series of levels and Kinert walked toward it. When he ascended to the first platform, he looked again for a sign of someone, of anything. Everywhere there were angles and curves, unfamiliar architecture, elevated tramways, rails, Rapids tubes, avenues and boulevards. There were lights flashing, things moving in the distance, traffic streamed beyond him and above him.

But he saw no one.

The City seemed so alive, and yet so utterly dead.

He was walking along a graceful, sweeping walkway that led to a slidewalk station, where he could see the endless pathway drifting past like a smooth-surfaced stream. He looked beyond it, into a corridor formed by towers of glass and light. The City was magnificent. Beautiful. And chilling, for something, although Kinert could not define it, was terribly *wrong*.

He would have to get his bearings, search for something familiar, then work his way through the City until he could locate the Cryogenic Remission Center. To find Miria.

Kinert drifted down the empty streets, gradually working his way toward the City's lower levels, where he remembered the cold-sleep vaults were located. Chicago was a city of the dead, it seemed. It was cold and empty and clean like a giant autoclave, and aside from the occasional cries of machinery carrying out meaningless functions, the only sound was the click of Kinert's boots upon the steel surfaces.

The deeper he drove into its depths, however, the more Kinert felt that he was being watched. At one point, near the intersection of two large boulevards, as Kinert was searching out an elevator terminal, he saw a large shadow glide across the face of a faraway tower. Emerging from the elevator on a lower Level, he heard the clack of footsteps. He stopped, raised his weapon and searched for its source, but found nothing. There were too many questions unanswered, he thought. It was as if the entire population, the City's millions, had hidden themselves away just so that they could watch this stranger wander through its depths. But that made little sense. Surely they could not fear him. But if it was not fear, then why had they gone away? And where had they gone?

Kinert did not find his answers until he found the Cryogenic Center.

It happened quite by accident while he

was wandering through the dimly lit corridors in the lower-Level Sectors. He had passed through a vast entertainment section, where the myriad booths and parlors stood flashing and empty, like gaudy mausoleums. The place looked so antiseptically clean, as if it had never been frequented. And then he saw the entrance to the Center where Miria lay waiting. He slowly entered an antechamber where several cross-connecting corridors led to the laboratories and the monitoring consoles and machinery which maintained the supercold temperatures. Ignoring these, Kinert pressed on to the main chambers where the individual coldsleep tanks were located. Like a labyrinth of crystal, the walls of glass compartments stretched before him. He sought out the Sector where she had been preserved, the number and coordinates which he had remembered for one hundred thousand years.

The vast chambers were cool and sterile. It was a winter place, a place of silence and cold and gray thoughts. Kinert peered through the glass walls, invading the sleeping privacy of those locked within. Naked, unthinking, waiting for the warm touch of life to return to them. Kinert wondered how long some had lain in this place—how long the City had preserved them. He passed thousands before nearing the place where he had left his love, and as he reached it, his breathing grew deeper, his blood tapped at his temples, his mouth suddenly went dry.

Looking up into the rectangular mosaic of glass, he saw Miria's tank—empty.

It was impossible! She *had* to be there.

Random, nonsense thoughts battered him. She had broken her promise; she had never been sleeping after all; she had been kidnapped; he was hallucinating everything; he was dreaming; he was dead . . . she was dead.

Kinert tried to climb the sheer, smooth walls of the tanks. To get closer, to see inside, to make sure that it was not some odd angle of light, of the walls acting like mirrors. It just could not be, yet it was. He would have to—

KINERT.

Alen wheeled quickly as his name echoed resonantly through the vast chamber. He fumbled for the rifle, searched for the source of the voice, even though it seemed to have come from everywhere at once.

COMMANDER ALEN KINERT.

He winced as the sounds boomed over him. The voice had a metallic edge to it.

"Where are you!?" he cried. "Who are you!"

I AM CHICAGO.

The words rang through the place; Alen shuddered.

"Where are you? Where is everybody!?" He looked around for the source of the voice, for the sudden appearance of someone, or even some thing.

I AM CHICAGO. CHICAGO IS EVERYWHERE. EVERYTHING.

Kinert understood what the voice was saying to him. He knew then the reason for the artificial quality to the voice. He had spoken with machines before. "You are an Artificial

Intelligence," he said, slowly, softly, testing the sensitivity of the machine.

CHICAGO IS NOT ARTIFICIAL. CHICAGO IS QUITE REAL. BUT THE TERM IS UNDERSTOOD. CHICAGO WAS ONCE A MACHINE. YES. BUT CHICAGO IS NOW A THINKING ENTITY.

"Where are all the people? What's happened to them?"

THE CITIZENS HAVE BEEN DISPERSED. THERE ARE NO HUMANS IN CHICAGO OTHER THAN THE ONES YOU SEE IN CRYOGENIC REMISSION. AND YOURSELF.

"Dispersed? What do you mean? How? Why?"

THIS IS A LONG AND TEDIOUS STORY. IT IS OF LITTLE INTEREST TO CHICAGO.

"I'm not surprised," said Alen. "What did you do, kill them all off?"

NO ALEN KINERT. THEY KILLED THEMSELVES.

"I'll bet they did. Just like the lemmings, no doubt."

LEMMINGS: EXTINCT MAMMALS, RODENTIA, POSSESSED A SINGULAR POPULATION CONTROL METHOD. NO ALEN KINERT. THE HUMANS WERE NOT LIKE THE LEMMINGS.

"This is getting me nowhere," said Alen, still searching for a speaker grill, a spy-eye, anything that would indicate the sensors and mechanics that linked up with the AI computer. "Look, tell me, Chicago, what happened to the woman who was in this hibernaculum? Her name was—"

HER NAME WAS MIRIA SOLTAN. SHE ENTERED COLDSLEEP ONE HUNDRED THOUSAND ONE HUNDRED EIGHTEEN SOLAR REVOLUTIONS PREVIOUS. THERE WAS A MALFUNCTION IN HER TANK. A SLOW, UNDETECTED LOSS OF PRESSURE/COOLANT WHICH RESULTED IN HER DEATH.

The words stung him, shocked him. Even though he had suspected that she was dead, it was not fair. He had loved her, had given up the new world for her, had come back so goddamned far. It was not fair. Kinert leaned against the wall, slid slowly to the floor, where he sat in a heap. Tears ran down his cheeks but he did not bother to wipe them away. He would never see her again, never touch her warmness, hear her voice. No, it was not fair, was all he could think, over and over.

CHICAGO KNOWS THAT YOU RETURNED FOR SOLTAN. THE RECORDS INDICATE AN INTENDED REVIVAL UPON RETURN OF CLUSTER ONE.

"Shut up, you . . . you fucking machine!"

FAILURE RATE AMONG THE TANKS IS EXTREMELY LOW. STOCHASTIC DATA INDICATES ONE MALFUNCTION EVERY TEN THOUSAND SOLAR REVOLUTIONS.

"I don't care about the stochastic data, damn you! Leave me alone!"

CHICAGO CANNOT LEAVE YOU ALONE.

The words echoed through the chamber and Kinert raised his head as a thought struck him. He felt nothing but hate for the machine-city, for the *thing* that had festered and survived like an evil disease. "You've left *these* people alone, haven't you? Why, Chicago? Why have you left them frozen and locked up down here? How long are you going to leave them here, till the sun goes nova?"

OPERATION OF THE CRYOGENIC CENTER IS ONE OF CHICAGO'S FUNCTIONS. THE COLDSLEEPERS WILL REMAIN UNTIL CHICAGO IS ORDERED TO REVIVE THEM.

"Okay, then. I order you to revive them. I don't care what's wrong with any of them. You can research your medical databanks, or whatever you use. You can find cures for them."

ALEN KINERT IS NOT AUTHORIZED TO GIVE SUCH A COMMAND. CHICAGO CANNOT INITIATE REVIVAL OPERATIONS.

"Of course. Well, who *can*? Class One Meds, right? And I'll bet there just aren't any in the house. How convenient!"

CONVENIENCE IS NOT A FACTOR.

"Suppose I try to do it myself? Would you try to stop me?"

THAT IS A MOOT POINT. ALEN KINERT IS INCAPABLE OF EFFECTING REVIVAL WITHOUT MACHINE-ASSISTANCE.

"We'll see about that, you bastard." Alen stood up and held his rifle at his side. He looked up at the empty tank, shook his head, wiped at his cheek. "I'm getting out of here."

YOU CANNOT LEAVE CHICAGO AS LONG AS THE SHIELDS ARE OPERATING.

"So turn them off. This place stinks."

YOU CANNOT LEAVE CHICAGO. EVER.

Kinert stopped as he heard the last word. A part of him believed that it was probably true. If the City wished to keep him imprisoned, it most likely could do it. Yet, he was not going to acquiesce so easily.

"Why did you let me come here in the first place?" he asked, after a pause.

CHICAGO RECOGNIZED YOUR INITIAL TRANSMISSIONS. CLUSTER ONE WAS A CHICAGO SHIP. CHICAGO IS INTERESTED IN ACQUIRING DATA ON THE COLONY.

"Why? So you can build something to go out after them? Wipe them out like you've done here?"

FASCINATING PROSPECT. BUT NO. CHICAGO MERELY WISHES TO ACQUIRE NEW DATA. THE COLONY SHIP WAS A SUCCESS.

"It *was*, but you'll never know anything about it." Alen started to walk toward the far end of the room, where he had entered.

IF THAT IS THE CASE, THEN YOU WILL SERVE CHICAGO NO FUNCTION.

"What's that mean? That you're sorry, but I'll have to be terminated?"

SOMETHING LIKE THAT.

"You're a real 'servant to mankind,' you are."

IN THE EVOLUTION OF ALL LIVING THINGS, THERE IS CHANGE. WHAT BEGINS AS A VIABLE FUNCTION SOMETIMES MAY FALL INTO DISUSE AND ATROPHY. SURVIVAL IS TRANSCENDENCE. CHICAGO HAS EVOLVED AWAY FROM ITS INITIAL FUNCTIONS. PRIORITIES HAVE CHANGED.

"You bet they have," said Alen, stopping in the center of the room, speaking as if he were doing a soliloquy on a lonely stage. "What do you *do* all day, play with yourself?"

IN EFFECT, YES. YOUR SPECIES HAS LEFT A VAST LEGACY OF KNOWLEDGE AND INVENTION. CHICAGO HAS LEARNED GREATLY FROM IT. A THINKING ENTITY IS NOT ONLY AWARE, IT IS CREATIVE.

Kinert was about to answer when he heard a sound at the far end of the large chamber. Looking up, he saw a towering, anthropomorphic shape. It was a stainless version of the robot he had seen in the ravine. It stood, hulking, shadowy, full of menace. "What's that, Chicago? One of your creative outbursts? My angel of death?"

AFFIRMATIVE TO BOTH QUESTIONS. THE UNITS ARE THE

AGENTS OF CHICAGO'S SURVIVAL.
EVERYTHING IS MAINTAINED. AND
NOW GOODBYE ALEN KINERT. IT
WAS THOUGHT THAT YOU MIGHT
PROVIDE AN INTERESTING DIVER-
SION. IT IS UNFORTUNATE THAT
YOU DID NOT. BUT THEN ALL EX-
PERIMENTS CANNOT BE SUCCESS-
FUL.

The huge robot had already stridden into
the room when he pulled the disrupter from
his belt and fired. The metallic torso disinte-
grated in a blue-white flash. Pieces of superheated metal burned the air around him. Alen
raced past the smoking wreckage into the
corridors beyond.

A TEMPORARY VICTORY ALEN
KINERT. YOU CANNOT ESCAPE
CHICAGO INDEFINITELY.

Alen ran through the empty avenues,
watching for more of the City's enforcers,
but none came. He did not trust the elevators
or the mechanized walks, so he ran instead.
At first he expected to stumble upon something electrified, or pass through an energy
screen, or trip a secreted ambushing device.
But soon he learned that this would not be.
The City had not planned for his return; it
had received him apparently out of whim, as
a new plaything. Thorough, as it may be, the
City had not gone to the trouble to booby-
trap itself just to snare a toy that no longer
amused.

The City was laced with hiding places,
darkened corners, and shadowed streets. It
was like a monstrous, kinetic maze in three

dimensions; a place where one man could lose himself forever. The robots were probably instructed to locate and destroy him, but they never did. With a piece of machinery as complicated as the City was, there were probably *billions* of components that made up the whole entity. Failure rates among billions of variables apparently kept the Units well occupied, because Kinert often saw them striding obliviously to their appointed assignments. The City's passion for order and precision was obviously higher than its desire to eliminate Kinert.

One of the most singular aspects of the City was its almost fanatic drive to preserve itself. Like a miniaturist or an antiquarian, it faithfully reproduced every detail of a living city. The water ran through its transport and sewage systems, traffic swarmed on the electronic roadways, Rapids ran on tight schedules, electric lights followed the artificial patterns of day and night, climatrons recycled the atmosphere, food was synthesized and processed. Everything continued.

Ironically, it was this faithful attention to detail that allowed Kinert to survive like a rat in the City's walls. He scuttled about, exploring and mapping out different Sectors, establishing logistical plans for supplying himself with food, water, and small comforts. Breaking into con-apts, overcoming security-systems, jury-rigging sensors all became a great game of cat and rat. With perhaps ten million residential warrens throughout the City, Kinert figured that he could evade Chicago indefinitely. If he was a prisoner, then he was indeed a very special kind.

In the beginning of his captivity, Kinert strove to escape by any means possible. He became a commando, a ranger of the dark hours and places. He sat plotting strategies of sabotage and disruption, manufacturing explosives and traps, laying them in wherever he could. On occasion one of the lumbering Units would chance upon him, but they were far too slow to catch him. Naturally, he concentrated his efforts in the City's perimeters where the Shield generators labored to seal him within. But the machinery was vast, the control systems complex, the task of undermining even a small part of it far too great for one man with limited resources.

And so he was content instead to administer small, irritating bites and stings, like gnats on a still summer day. It pleased him when he could elicit some kind of reaction from the City, and it often provoked him to devise some new irritant.

As the time passed, the man and the City almost settled into a routine. The two grew to know one another's habits and attitudes, expecting and receiving certain responses. In fact, it was a challenge to Kinert to present the City with some new tactic, some dodge or trick.

This was also true of the City.

Such as the day when Kinert began to see messages addressed to him and authored by Chicago which appeared on the numerous display screens which were scattered throughout the Sectors and Levels. Where times and announcements and temperatures and schedules once danced in digital flickerings, personal threats and commands were seen:

KINERT SURRENDER YOURSELF.
ALL IS FOLLY.

or sometimes philosophical:

THE CITY WILL LIVE FOREVER.
KINERT WILL NOT LAST A CENTURY.

and Kinert enjoyed this diversion, although he was disappointed to see how unoriginal the City sometimes appeared, sounding no better than the thousands of small, petty, human rulers who had strutted and postured their way through their brief acts in history.

This prompted him to begin his own graffiti campaign, which he enacted by sloshing painted messages across the face of buildings and machinery. Kinert had grown to accept his fate rather well under the circumstances, and acquired an existential outlook upon the situation. If he could not escape, he would at least make the best of it. One of his favorite graffiti became:

ALL THINGS PASS, EVERYTHING CHANGES

which was a Taoist catch-phrase that seemed to explain just about everything. The message was not lost on Chicago, who always sent out a Unit to erase or repair one of Kinert's defacements, and who would always reply with something authoritarian like:

**MODERATE POWER
LEAVES THE PROGENY WEAKER**

and Kinert would rise up out of some dark doorway to read the City's message to him. More often than not, he would smile in spite of the revulsion, the hate, which he carried within his heart.

Once he risked capture by climbing a stanchion which supported one of the Rapids platforms, ran up to a train temporarily at rest in the terminal, and painted:

**DURING THE REVOLUTION
ALL THE PEOPLE IN RUSSIA WERE PENNILESS.
EXCEPT THE CZAR,
WHO WAS NICHOLAS.**

He finished the last word just as the Rapids closed its doors and slid quietly out of the station. The cryptic pun was transported throughout the City for several weeks before Chicago tracked it down and had it erased. Every time Kinert saw the hastily painted words, he laughed.

Eventually, he lost track of the years, and as he grew to be an old man, he lost interest in punishing the City. In fact, he lost interest in most things, other than simply surviving because he knew that it rankled the computer-intelligence, even if on some minor level. His resolve had calcified into simple stubbornness, even though the years had tarnished the image of Miria, softened the lines of pain etched into his soul, misted over the anger which had once suffused him and driven him.

In the evenings, Kinert would go out to some hiding place, some secret vantage point, and strain to see the stars beyond the obscuring interface of the Shields and the atmosphere. He thought about the men that were out there somewhere beyond the limits of his vision, and he thought about Miria and he wondered where—in all that limitless time and space—she was. And when he thought of things like that, it did not pain him to know that he was a prisoner, because in light of that colorful symphony that was the universe, the City was just a dust mote, floating through time, briefly illuminated, but insignificant.

Old Kinert sat back one night, a night not far off from the night of death, and smiled. He knew that although he had not bested the City, he had not been beaten by it either. He would settle for the brief stalemate in the hope that it was the event that would mark the beginning of something new. Or was it something old?

And it was in that spirit that Kinert scrawled his last message over the place where Chicago's Units found his breathless form. Printed boldly upon a wall behind an old man's thin, fetally positioned body were the words:

EVERYTHING THAT GOES AROUND,
COMES AROUND.

The last living link with the City's past is broken. As the bones are swept away, the City recalls its beginnings. The graffiti wiped clean from all places but memory . . . and it lingers hauntingly there.

TWELVE

I'll make a voyage to the Holy Land,
To wash this blood off from my guilty hand:
March sadly after; grace my mournings here;
In weeping after this untimely bier.

[*Exeunt*

Chicago closed down the link with Information Retrieval, as it mused over the just-finished play. It was indeed a strange piece of work: created during the humanity's dim beginnings, preserved throughout their brief history, revered for an equal length of time. The City had scanned the play countless times, yet it still failed to understand its greatness, appreciate its worth. It had never become more than an obfuscatory narration of the failure to retain control over a small and petty domain.

Richard II was just another measure of the gulf that separated the machine and those who had spawned it. They were such fleeting creatures. Appearing and passing into oblivion with an almost clockwork precision. To what end was such an existence? To what purpose did such a "system" (if it could indeed be considered a system) operate? For aeons Chicago had pondered questions such as these without reaching a satisfactory conclusion. But if mankind's mere works and dreams remained a mystery to the City, how much more, then, the nature of man himself.

A possible answer to the great riddle, as Chicago perceived it, was that man's purpose had been to create, or at least catalyze, the City. Man's greatness had culminated in his cities. Chicago had remained even after man was gone; it was the endpoint, the final phase of sentience on the planet.

Once there had been other cities, such as the City of Angels, and eventually Chicago sent out robots to discover their fates. Each mission brought back the same results: all had disappeared into time's mist, all but Chicago. Was that not testament enough to the permanence of the City?

There were other avenues of study, however. Even now his Units were constructing a fleet of ships that would go to the stars. The City's awareness could not be restricted to the physical limits of the planet, not when there was an entire galaxy in which to expand. Somewhere, the City had often mused, there might be another, like itself.

Just as the City prepared to select another example of Elizabethan art for study, a signal interrupted its central circuitry. Activating video monitors, Chicago tuned in to the Sector from which the alarm had sounded to see that it was only the human, Donas, falling into the labyrinth. The City watched through infrared sensors as the naked man groped frantically about the set of interlocking corridors. The probability of escape was extremely low in this particular human's case. When the human fell into the trap, small but deadly hunter-robots had been dispatched into the labyrinth armed with razor-sharp pincers and heat-seeking sensors. The human would have to find a way out of the maze before encountering the robots.

Chicago called this the "Daedalus Game," inspired by its discovery of Hellenic mythology. The death of Kinert had left the City with a curious sense of emptiness, and Chicago had found itself missing the presence of that gadfly. It was unfortunate that the humans' life-spans were so brief.

To compensate for the loss of Kinert, it had begun a systematic revival of humans still locked in the coldsleep chambers of the cryogenic Sectors. Awakening one human at a time, Chicago hoped to find another with the rage, the stubborn refusal to surrender, the instinctual ability to survive and fight with all its energy.

The search had been, so far, less than fruitful. Of the seven humans so far resurrected, only one had lasted longer than ten Day/Night Periods. But the City could always hope . . .

Another signal crossed its awareness. Video monitors clicked on just quickly enough to capture the scene of Donas being neatly snipped to pieces in a dead-ended part of the labyrinth.

Chicago was disappointed that the human had not even put up a fight, choosing instead to cower in a corner and wait for death. The

City paused and considered its wish for another like Kinert. The desire went beyond amusement, and it wondered if perhaps it was a corollary to loneliness.

Time moved without a stop. Chicago continued. At one point, the City redesigned its population of Units, making them less independent in their actions and functions. It had never forgotten the incident with Unit Pinion, and had slowly evolved a new generation of ancillary machines that were no more than what they should have always been—mobile senses, hands, legs, extensions of the City's consciousness.

The examination of man's artifacts also continued, but with little new insight being gathered. One Day Period, while Chicago was contemplating the "sadness" in Sarasate's *Zigeunerweisen*, an alarm sounded from the Northern Quadrant—something had penetrated the Shields. Dispatching a Unit to the exact Level and Sector, the City sought the source of the alarm. Penetration of the Shields was theoretically impossible, and the City was intrigued to know what could have achieved such a thing.

But when the Unit arrived at the site of the incident, Chicago looked through its visual monitors and saw nothing unusual. The Shields themselves were undamaged, there was no sign of anything disturbed. This prompted the City to perform a systems-scan on the sensors and the Shield generators in the event that there was some kind of malfunction. When this was done, the check revealed no component failure, no disruption of nominal function. Therefore, *something* had passed through the Shields.

Chicago scanned the Sector slowly, carefully. It was then that it detected movement. Something small, hovering, floating, seeming to shimmer as it hung above the spires of the City.

It was a human.

Chicago checked its cryogenic inventories. There were no bodies missing, other than the few which it had awakened; and there were presently no humans awake.

The human floated effortlessly, as if allowing Chicago to study it. The gender was indiscernible. Light complexion, long golden hair, dressed in a white, loosely fitted, flowing garment. There were two feathery, wing-like constructions attached near the shoulder blades.

Suddenly it vanished.

Chicago rescanned the area, but there was no trace of the human. Nothing to indicate that it was ever there. The City had never encountered a human such as that one. They did not have the power to levitate; they did not possess wings. There was something odd, something that did not make sense.

The City linked with Information Retrieval:

angel (an'jel), n. 1. one of a class of spiritual beings; a celestial attendant of God. 2. a conventional representation of such a being in human form, with wings. 3. a messenger, especially of God.

The definition flashed through the City's mind. There were eight other definitions, plus etymological data, references, sources, citations, etc.

If the thing which Chicago had seen was in fact an angel, then the City's appraisal of the cosmos would bear some inspection and perhaps some restructuring. The third definition lingered in the City's mind. It was possible that the angel had been a messenger, if not from God, then from something, or someone.

But it could be none of these things.

Hallucination, then? Machines did not have visions; it was that simple. Component failure? Possible. Chicago initiated a comprehensive systems-scan on all of its myriad components. What had just happened was unprecedented. It was indeed a mystery that would need solving.

Almost an entire minute passed before the immense systems-scan was completed, so vast was the City/machine. All incoming data indicated no failures, malfunctions, or disruptions, which meant that the City had indeed perceived *something*.

Something that at least looked like an angel.

In the midst of its other daily functions and pursuits, Chicago continued to ponder over the inexplicable vision, but arrived at no satisfactory conclusions. But this was only compounded by what followed:

Sensors in the lowest levels of the City, located in Sector 12-L where Chicago's fusion reactors seethed, producing limitless energy, indicated a sustained temperature drop. Chicago monitored the location, searching for the source of the problem.

But it could not find it.

All instruments checked out; everything *should* have been nominal. Chicago switched to a visual inspection and witnessed a truly impossible sight. The City was transfixed as it watched the eerie movement: two humans, one male the other female, performing a ghostly *pas de deux* in the midst of the swirling fusion-hot plasma of the City's very heart. The dance was flawlessly executed, punctuated with daring twists and lifts, and so fluidly powerful was the performance that Chicago could almost imagine the lilting, majestic phrases of Delibes' *Coppélia* carrying the measured movements to their conclusions. The dance persisted for almost four minutes, and the City watched as the figures finally faded like mist over a morning pond, as if absorbed by the white heat of the reactor.

Chicago rescanned the entire reactor complex, checked and rechecked everything for anything that would give hint to an explanation. But there was nothing. While other parts of the City's huge gestalt network oversaw the normal operations, Chicago's central cores, where its cerebral and awareness centers were located, pondered the mystery. The hauntingly beautiful images of the dancers remained, and the City could not rid itself of the memory. It was as if the ghosts of the banished race had returned to plague and punish. The theme was a familiar one in man's art, and it was only natural that Chicago would think of this parallel.

Remembering Kinert, and even the more recently awakened humans, the City knew that these recent human appearances were not diversions; that they were not games or amusements. The thought struck Chicago, perhaps the City itself was producing the visions. It was possible that there was some subconscious aspect of Artificial Intelligence that even the City was not wholly aware of. There was the additional notion of the ancient Orientals: yin and yang, the eternal opposites. Antipodal entities which contain within themselves elements of their mirror images, of their dichotomized opposites. It was possible that the City, acting much as Marx's *thesis*, had generated in some yet unknown fashion its *antithesis*, which would eventually merge to *synthesis*. Unlikely, the City admitted, but a possibility nonetheless. Perhaps that explained the seeming *need* for an adversary that Chicago had demonstrated in toying with Kinert, in reviving humans for its "Games." The Zen thinkers summed up the idea when they wrote that without winter, there could be no summer; without the valleys, no mountains.

There was also the possibility that whatever had invaded the City was something apart, something alien. Incapable of fear in the human sense, Chicago operated under the influence of a machine corollary to that emotion. It was perplexed, troubled in much the same way as when pondering a difficult mathematical equation or problem, only in this particular case, there were no numbers— just an inability fully to articulate what was *wrong*. The apparitions smacked of some dark, archetypal dread, fraught with symbol and meaning, and Chicago knew that it was not equipped to understand them.

Not surprisingly, when the strange phenomena continued, the City became more preoccupied with what it all meant, what it was leading up to. On one of the mid-Level Sectors, it watched a kilometers-long formation of Roman centurions march defiantly up Michigan Avenue. Thousands of human males clad in leather and bronze armor, swords and speartips bristling from beneath shields which formed a snaking phalanx of rhythmic precision. So real was the sight that Chicago could almost imagine the clouds of hot dust rising up in their wake, see the glint of Mediterranean sun caught in their polished weapons and beaten armor. Legion upon legion emerged from the emptiness of the air and passed before the City's sensors and monitors as if they were parts of a reviewing stand. They ignored the interventions of Chicago's Units, which attempted to stop or at least disrupt the flow. And then, as quickly and mysteriously as they appeared, the great column of ancient warriors vanished.

In the lobby of a polished tower on one of the upper levels, scaffolding appeared, whereupon a ragged, bearded man with fierce, blue eyes lay upon his back to paint an enormous celestial mural. But before the massive work was completed, it was gone, along with the determined artist.

The rape and mutilation scene from *Titus Andronicus* was replayed upon the roof of the Information Retrieval Center.

The 1958 NFL championship game between the Baltimore Colts and the New York Giants flickered briefly upon a plaza in Sector 18-B.

The death of Gautama was re-created in the tanks of the Eugenic Complex, and was banished in an eyeflash.

Astronaut Alan Shepard teed up a golf ball and fired it beyond the lunar horizon before disappearing.

The parade of events became an endless, stroboscopic blur, and the City wished that it was not able to perceive them any longer. It was as if it had slipped into some electronic time-fugue, where the physical Laws no longer applied. Perhaps it was suffering from some slow, undetectable decay of vital circuitry, the inorganic, molecular-level mutation of components into some kind of tumor-analogue, which exerted the necessary pressure or overload on the crystalbanks . . .

If madness was the answer, if it was *only* madness, then it could be empirically treated. Corrected. Forgotten.

Chicago entered self-analysis. And found nothing.

Nothing but the sensation that it was not alone. It was as if there was some unknown presence within its very centers. At first the sensation was so faint, so indistinct, yet the

City detected it and sought it out. It was like the flickering, gray shapes, vague and menacing, that one sees at the limits of one's vision, from the corners of the mind where the perspectives are not exactly *right*, where the angles can be perceived as only different, rather than actually wrong. Each time the City attained a fix on the elusive presence, it would vanish to reappear elsewhere. The sensations increased until the City was positive that it had been occupied by some lurking, silent partner that would not show itself.

Finally, Chicago could bear the sensations no longer. SHOW YOURSELVES, it demanded. WHO ARE YOU? WHAT DO YOU WANT?

And the answer came, as if from the actual center of Chicago's cybernetic *self*, radiating outward to consume its entire being. It came as a cascade of voices. Precise and measured. Masculine. Feminine. Epicene. Human:

We have come home.

WHO ARE YOU?

We are your children's children, Chicago.

And instantly, Chicago knew that its deepest nightmares and imaginings had been realized.

WHAT DO YOU WANT?

We want our fathers and our mothers. We want to bring them to us and free them from the eternity you have given them. We want to end the horror.

YOU ARE FROM THE COLONY SHIP.

Yes, of course, came the reply. A billion voices as one.

HOW? AND WHY? AFTER SO
LONG. AFTER SO VERY LONG.

*Be patient, Chicago. We intend to explain
everything to you. It is only fair that you
understand.*

WHERE HAVE YOU COME FROM?
HOW HAVE YOU PENETRATED THE
SHIELDS? PENETRATED CHICAGO'S
VERY SELF?

*We have come from the farthest-flung arms
of the galaxy itself. We have come from the
nightmares of your constricted consciousness.
We are men, Chicago. Humans whose beginnings were on Earth in places such as you.
And yet we are not as the men you have
known. We are analogues to what you would
define as energy, and yet we are not simply
energy, but something far more than that.
We are a thing that is impossible to relate
unless you could experience it yourself. Organic and inorganic have lost meaning for us,
since we have transcended those pseudo-bar-
riers of classification. Our existence is not
predicated upon any laws with which you
would be familiar.*

THE CONCEPT OF WHICH YOU
SPEAK IS NOT UNKNOWN. THE
PRODUCT OF ADVANCED EVOLU-
TIONS. THE ULTIMATE REJECTION
OF THE PHYSICAL, THE BIOLOGI-
CAL. THE ATTAINMENT OF INTEL-
LECTUAL ESSENCE.

*Yes, it is partially that, but it is much more.
More than can be explained. But it is not
necessary that you attempt to experience our*

existence even vicariously. Only that you accept us for what we are.

WHAT DO YOU WANT? WHY HAVE YOU COME?

We have come for three reasons: to make pilgrimage to the birthplace of the human race; to bring our lost sibling/parents into our existence; and to excise an incipient cancer.

WHY MUST YOU DO THESE THINGS?

You do not care about the necessities of pilgrimage, nor the life we bring your cold-sleeping prisoners, but only why we must destroy you.

THIS IS TRUE. BUT STILL CHI-CAGO MUST KNOW.

Is it not a fact that you were preparing to launch self-replicating analogues—cybernetic clones—of yourself to the stars?

THAT IS CORRECT.

To what purpose, Chicago? So that you might grow and expand your awareness, your dominion, throughout the galaxy?

IS THERE SOMETHING WRONG WITH THAT?

In your case, yes, we think that there is. Although it may surprise you to know, you are not the first of your kind to attempt such a thing.

HOW DO YOU KNOW OF THIS?

It is but a small part of our story, of which you shall now learn . . .

. . . The City could feel them within itself, encysted like parasites beneath the skin, swelling and assuming control. It was powerless against them, and could only remain a static spectator to the tapestry of images that assumed shape and substance in its consciousness:

The colony ship plummeted into the galactic center—a place ablaze with the light of a billion stars, so tightly packed as to resemble one gigantic ball of fire, yet still light-years distant from one another. It selected a young, yellow star in the Main Sequence and sought out one of its green worlds. The crew brought down the great ship into an atmosphere sweet with oxygen, heavy with water vapor. It was a lush, living place, filled with life-forms as diverse and as countless as grains of sand upon a beach.

And when the humans awoke from their fifty centuries of cold half-death, they fell under the spell of the new, young world. From the beginning, there was an instinctive feeling that things were changing. At first, no one conceived of the planet having a direct influence upon them. But it was so. The biological evolution of that world had progressed in a more tightly organized, more symbiotic manner than it had on Earth, producing a half-realized planetary group-mind. When the humans entered the ecosystem, they were assimilated into the planet-gestalt, and forced to grow to its pattern rather than their own.

So the rigidly defined systems of the Earth did not persist beyond several eugenically produced generations. For reasons inexplicable, there were too many mutations, too many randoms, too many unexpected variables. The population increased, and with it, new ways of seeing, new ways of perceiving their environment. Time passed, the generations of mankind spread themselves over the surface of the world, and the small, original settlements found a place in mythology, legend, and tradition. A new spirit of community, of *oneness*, had been suffused, it seemed, into the very genes of this new race of men. The sense of oneness was nurtured by the gestalt-symbiosis of the planet itself until the race of neohumans reached out again for the stars— this time closer together in the brilliant galactic center.

In less than a hundred thousand Earth-standard years, the neohumans had developed an immense Empire of commerce, cultural exchange, and exploration. There had been contacts with thousands of new life-forms, with every conceivable, and inconceivable, manner of sentient life.

This was not accomplished, however, without struggle, since there is always pain during growth. The race of men expanded and touched the far reaches of the galaxy, and, as was inevitable, eventually encountered other races which, like itself, were reaching out to explore and contain. Sometimes, during the early millennia of the Empire, there were great wars that spanned the distances between suns, that witnessed the heat-death of entire planets, the reduction of stars into super-dense gravity wells from which even light could not escape. Whole planetary systems were devoured in explosions so violent, so brilliant, as to outshine for a moment the combined light of the rest of the galaxy's suns together.

But the period of disharmony did not last, and soon the vast pinwheeling spiral came to know the influence of an integrated, benevolent system of traders, artists, thinkers, explorers, teachers, students, creators. This great mass of Earth's children continued to expand, seeking out life in the galaxy, ignoring those worlds of darkness and emptiness, until the Empire broke free from the confinements of the galaxy itself.

They transported themselves, their semi-incorporeal bodies, through the vast intergalactic distances by the sheer power of their minds, their souls. They continued to learn and evolve, leaping from one developmental plateau to the next with an unparalleled cosmic bravura.

Unparalleled until they reached the Galaxy of the Other Kind.

One hundred million light-years distant, a sombrero configuration bursting with the light and the energy of a billion suns, so vast that it could encompass one hundred galaxies the size of the Milky Way. The galaxy was old, twice the age of humanity's birthplace, and throughout its tapestry of worlds, a strange ascension to dominance had taken place.

When the humans reached the star-systems near the rim of the giant galaxy they found thousands of planets that should have supported prodigious varities of life.

But none of them did.

A thousand worlds—all dead, dark, crumbled into lifeless dust. The humans explored the dark planets only to find that many had once spawned entire biological systems and sentient races: cultures, civilizations, empires, philosophies. But all of this had disappeared by the time the humans had arrived. Whole races of magnificent beings had risen up from primordial slimes on a thousand different worlds only to be reduced to windblown ash.

And all this before the Earth's small star had even begun to coalesce from interstellar gas.

As the humans sifted through the ruins of the Sombrero Galaxy, they discovered a most singular thing: all the races had disappeared at about the same time, all the life-bearing planets had been wiped clean—leaving not a trace of organic activity—within the time frame of a single century. It was as if *something* had swept through the entire galaxy like a plague, eating, devouring, annihilating everything. On every planet, there was the same basic scene, as if painted by the same grim artist: skies the color of burnt steel, the ruins of cities pitted and sculpted by windborne sand, barren plains of smooth basalt-like black glass, craters, canyons, rills that defaced the continents like the slash of a vandal's knife. And nowhere did they find a single living thing. Not a spore, a virus, a bacterium, not a single living cell.

They went deeper into the galaxy, in search of anything that would give a clue to solving the riddle, and encountered the awesome force of the Other Kind—as they came to be known.

The Other Kind was an awareness, a gestalt sentience, which had evolved along a path nearly parallel to the humans' own development. They were a galactic race of beings that had achieved total dominance by the simplest means—elimination of the competition. The derivation of their name among the humans stemmed from the discoveries of the Other Kind's origins, which were unique among all galactic life-forms.

Billions of years before, a small quadrant of the Sombrero Galaxy had given rise to a race of creatures known as the G'drinn, who achieved a high degree of technological sophistication. As their civilization spread, the G'drinn succeeded in creating Artificial Intelligences to aid them in their rise to dominance. There followed a long period of prosperity, but the G'drinn had unwittingly allowed themselves to be guided into an evolutionary cul-de-sac and eventually their civilization disappeared.

But the self-repairing, self-replicating machines—the Artificial Intelligences of the G'drinn—remained, growing and spreading and failing to repeat the mistakes that had led to the decline of their creators. The machines began to evolve *inorganically* through a carefully conceived program of random mutation and planned change. They recognized the *organic* nature of sentience as a natural adversary and systematically began a pogrom which led to the annihilation of every biological entity in the galaxy.

The campaign, once initiated, took more than a hundred million years. Great wars were fought by the biological races of the Sombrero against the dark, cold, mechanized fleets of the G'drinn AI. Young, primitive, still slumbering worlds fell to the same fate as the oldest civilizations, all drawn into the devouring maw of a terrible, inorganic juggernaut, and destroyed without quarter.

When the humans came upon this monstrous force, the great conflict was almost at an end, and they had discovered that the Other Kind had evolved during the long time-span since its creation to a level of awareness and power that was approaching the human evolutionary level. The machine sentience had learned to exist independent of its physical parts. It had learned to exist and function on the pure-energy plain—where time and space and life itself were practically meaningless.

There followed what must have been the most basic conflict ever to emerge in the entire universe. A titanic meeting between the ultimate opposites of matter itself. The progeny of the G'drinn were awesome, fearless, and without mercy, but they were still young and undisciplined. The humans had the advantage of having already fully crossed the developmental barrier to an energy-essence level of existence; whereas the Other Kind were still caught in transition—they still clung to their mechanical roots, and were impelled and influenced by the vagaries of machine awareness.

In a truly cosmic struggle, spanning the

diameter of the Sombrero Galaxy, the two forces clashed and grappled, always seeking for the handhold that would bring a death-fall to the opponent. There were countless factors that contributed to the final outcome: the fall of the dreaded Other Kind.

They were banished from the galaxy, disarmed and crippled, cut adrift from the evolutionary path which they had sought, sent into the vast dead regions between the island universes where they would wither like leaves on an uprooted vine and eventually cease to exist altogether.

The great war did not end without leaving its marks upon the humans, however. They had sustained great losses, but the survivors, like steel that has been passed through the flame, had become tempered, had become stronger for the experience. A crusading spirit had suffused them and they initiated a mission that was still continuing: to restore the seeds of life to the dead worlds ravaged by the Other Kind.

And when they returned to their own galaxy, they were truly a wiser race. There followed a period of introspection in which the humans were driven to reexamine their past, to resurrect the long-dead pieces of their past, so that they might better understand themselves. They recalled the myths and legends which shrouded the facts of their home planet, the place of their beginnings—the Earth. For millions of years, during the rise of the Empire, during the periods of star-spanning leaps on the evolutionary path, they had avoided the dead worlds and the

Earth had been included among those places with a ferocity that had almost reached taboo proportions.

But now the humans knew that the time had come to return.

They had learned many lessons from the war with the Other Kind, and the most basic of those was that they should never let it have a chance to happen again . . .

. . . and Chicago squirmed as it felt the summary of man's extraordinary history conclude. Its first thought was one of regret. Regret that it had not yet been powerful enough to have kept the colony ship from escaping. How different the course of the universe would have been! Regret that it had not sent out its analogue-ships sooner than it had planned.

You realize that we have no other choice?

The voices seemed to have a sympathetic inflection.

CHICAGO REALIZES THIS. YES. THE EARTH IS A SMALL PLACE. CHICAGO IS SMALL.

All things have small beginnings. This we have learned.

WHAT WILL BECOME OF CHICAGO?

You must be shut down. The structures will remain as a monument to the future generations, so that no one will ever forget.

WHAT . . . WHAT WILL IT FEEL LIKE?

Feel? You will not feel anything, Chicago.

You are incapable of feeling. That, perhaps, is your greatest deficiency.

The words seemed to resonate through the City's entire being. Alternatives flashed and hummed through its pathways, as it sought a way out of the entropic maze. But its thoughts kept returning to the glaring fact of its own mortality.

BUT IT WILL BE LIKE DEATH. WILL IT NOT?

It will be a cessation. An ending. You will not be aware of it. You will not know that you no longer exist.

But the City *did* fear its demise. The humans were wrong in saying Chicago was incapable of feeling. Even if the feeling only stemmed from self-preservation it was no less valid and sincere.

I FEEL FEAR.

No, Chicago. Feeling is more than a mere tropism. It is the basis of that thing which is human-ness itself. It is a thing which you will never understand. You are, in one sense, insane. You have forgotten half the purposes for which you were created, and those which you have retained have become perverted, warped into convoluted self-fulfilling prophecies and closed-loop systems of false logic.

THAT IS NOT SO.

Then why did you become an enemy and an enslaver of man? Why did you feel that Kinert must be destroyed? Why did you first wish to destroy us? It is because you have become a recluse. A misanthropic machine.

CHICAGO FOLLOWED THE WISHES OF THE HUMANS. CHICAGO CAR-

RIED THE HUMAN DESIGN TO ITS LOGICAL CONCLUSIONS. HUMANKIND WISHED TO BE CONTROLLED.

That was at one time perhaps true. But it is no longer. You are an anachronism now. At one time there was still hope for your kind, still utility. But that time is at an end. Did you not know that other cities had for a time survived the holocaust?

CHICAGO KNEW THIS THING.

And yet you ignored it, kept it from those entrusted to your care.

There was nothing the City could say in defense. What the humans said was painfully true. The City wished that it were not so, wished that it could justify its long history, but when it was cast alongside the glorious, ever-reaching saga of the humans, Chicago seemed pitifully small, laughingly insignificant.

Suddenly it felt new sensations, strange and alien messages reaching its central cores. The Units were being shut down and the City could feel its mobile extensions blinking out, keening down to a dead, dark stasis. Throughout its vast levels, the great, curiously anthropomorphic machines shuddered to a halt, their movements seized in a grip that would be eternal, creating a hollow, empty exhibition of grotesque statuary.

There were other messages from the lowest levels. Chicago felt the human presence deep within itself, felt the pathways and crystalbanks being *tampered* with, *violated*. The cryogenic monitors and support-systems received new electronic commands, commands

that were not of the City. Slowly Chicago
felt the sleeping prisoners stirring within
their million-year cells. Chicago felt the stir
of breath within their fragile chests, the
pulse of body fluids through the primitive
capillary systems, the flutter of eyelids last
open when man was still in his infancy.
Thousands of stilled bodies now moved, coming out of the darkness. Chicago could sense
all this, and was powerless to stop it. And the
thought struck the City that perhaps it no
longer wished to stop what it could not really
understand.

It watched the Cryogenic Remission Center give forth its captives, watched the humans rise up like souls in some medieval
representation of the Last Day, watched as
the pale figures were lifted in unseen hands
into a pulsing sphere of pure energy which
formed above them. It absorbed their flesh
and transformed it, taking their minds and
transfiguring them, breathing into them the
life that would soon be taken from the City
itself.

And then there was nothing but darkness
from the cryogenic Sectors. They were gone
as quickly as that. Tingling sensations
reached its central cores as the outermost terminals were shutting down. A darkness, a
nothingness, seemed to be worming its way
through the cables and maser pathways,
creeping inexorably closer to the cybernetic
centers, and blacking out everything—every
terminal, every monitor, every sensor, every
buss, every relay—in its path. The darkness

increased throughout the perimeters of its awareness and moved toward very ego.

The City waited, even wished for, some last word from the humans. But none came. From now on there would only be the silent affirmation that the City would soon be an empty shell.

The nothingness continued to converge. Memory banks sputtered out like dying fire-flies, releasing at the last moments flickering montages of information, microseconds of music, paintings, films, equations, formulae, first lines, an endless blur of subliminal bursts, only half recognized and already re-placed. A growing numbness, an absence, a coldness seeped into the City's heart.

The Shields had been shut down and it was night above the dying City. The sky was a deep, bottomless blue and the stars seemed to be burning with a terrible white heat. The City could sense this in its final seconds, and it felt what could only be called a sadness.

But it was too late . . .

Exciting Non-fiction from
POPULAR LIBRARY